A Branching Narrative

Monuments

Simon Birks

A Branching Narrative
Monuments

First Edition

First Published in the UK by Blue Fox Publishing Limited
Text Copyright © Simon Birks 2024
Illustrations Copyright © Willi Roberts 2024
Cover Copyright © Lyndon White 2024

The right of Simon Birks to be identified as the author of this work has been asserted by him in accordance with the Copyright, Designs and Patent Act 1988

All rights reserved. No part of this publication may be reproduced, stored in a retrieval system, or transmitted, in any form, or by any means (electronic, mechanical, photocopying, recording or otherwise) without the prior written permission of the publisher.

This book is sold subject to the condition that it shall not, by way of trade or otherwise, be lent, hired out, or otherwise circulated without the publisher's prior consent in any form of binding or cover other than that in which it is published and without a similar condition being imposed on the subsequent purchaser.

Visit https://abranchingnarrative.substack.com/subscribe to read more of our adventures.

For Dad

None of us completely control the choices we make, and in the end, it is our actions that truly define us.

Thank you for your love, support and encouragement.

It was everything.

Contents

Welcome to Monuments	7
Paragraphs	8
Attributes	9
Testing Attributes	10
Weapons & Combat	11
Equipment & Weight	12
Rations	12
Adventure Sheet	14
Equipment Sheet	15
Encounter Sheet	16
Encounter Sheet	17
Adventure 01: The Watchtower	19
Adventure 02: Vents!	85
Adventure 03: Entombed!	173

Welcome to
Monuments: A Branching Narrative

A Branching Narrative is my Substack newsletter, offering monthly interactive fiction adventures.

You never know where the next adventure will take you or what the next mission will be!

The rules will roughly be the same each time, with perhaps a new rule or two if required by the situation. Every free subscriber gets access to the first room, which will be 25+ paragraphs.

Paying subscribers get the whole adventure, which will be at least 125 paragraphs!

You must use your experience, stealth, power, speed, accuracy, and detection to help you successfully navigate the locations and people encountered. Not all are enemies, and it is up to you to choose who to trust and who to fight.

You probably won't make it through on your first attempt (nor second, nor third), but don't despair! Re-start the mission and forge a new path toward your goal.

So, without further ado, let's teach you the basics so you can dive in as quickly as possible!

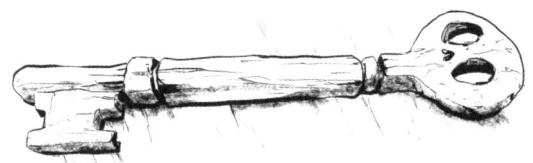

Paragraphs

New to gamebooks? Let us help you. Also known as interactive fiction, a gamebook is a multi-threaded story, which allows the player (you!) to make decisions for the protagonist (also you!).

Each section of text (aka a paragraph) has a number before it. The first, and starting, paragraph of the book is numbered **1**. The paragraphs that follow it are sequentially numbered but do not follow on. If you tried to read it like a normal book, it wouldn't make any sense.

At the end of each paragraph, you will be faced either with:

- a) No choice (you have died)
- b) Return to the paragraph you noted previously.
- c) One choice, turn to **n** paragraph.
- d) Or a series of two or more choices

In the instance of d), you get to choose the next action. Read the paragraph text fully; in places, the book is written with subtle clues as to the possible outcomes of the actions.

Once you have chosen, find the paragraph with the same number as your choice and continue from there!

In some paragraphs you will find objects, test attributes and fight against other enemies. Rules for each are on the following pages.

Attributes

You have 6 attributes, listed below with the appropriate method of calculation. Record the attributes on the adventure sheet.

1. *Health* – you begin the adventure with 30 *Health*. *Health* will reduce as you encounter enemies and traps along the way and is increased by resting or eating when not in battle.

2. *Speed* – how quickly you react and run. *Speed* is calculated as 1D6+6 (minimum 7, maximum 12).

3. *Accuracy* – how precise you are in aim and movement. *Accuracy* is calculated as 1D6+6 (minimum 7, maximum 12).

4. *Stealth* – how quietly you move and how well you hide. *Stealth* is calculated as 1D6+6 (minimum 7, maximum 12).

5. *Detection* – how efficient you are at detecting traps and reading the situation. *Detection* is calculated as 1D6+6 (minimum 7, maximum 12).

6. *Power* – how much force you can apply. *Power* is calculated as 1D6+6 (minimum 7, maximum 12).

Apart from *Health*, most attributes remain static unless you are injured, impaired, or improved during the adventure. Your attributes can exceed their starting level.

Whenever points are *restored* to an attribute, including *Health*, it may not go over the starting value. If the current value is equal to or higher than the starting value, nothing happens.

Testing Attributes

Whilst navigating your latest adventure, you will find many paragraphs asking you to test one of your attributes.

To test an attribute:

1. Roll 2D6.
2. If the result is equal to or **lower** than the attribute being tested, the test is successful.
3. If the result is **higher** than the attribute, the test is unsuccessful.
4. The paragraph will let you know what happens as a result of the test.
5. Sometimes, being unsuccessful has hidden benefits.

For example:

You are instructed to test your *Stealth*, which is currently at 8. You roll 2D6, and the result is 8. As the result is the same as your current total, the test is successful.

If you'd rolled 9 or more, the test would have been unsuccessful.

Weapons & Combat

The mission will tell you what weapons you have, how much damage they inflict, and how exactly you use them.

These combat rules will cover most of the combat you'll encounter within the missions.

1. Whoever has the highest *Speed* goes first. If tied, compare the two *Accuracy* attributes next. If these two numbers are also the same, compare *Health*. If these are equal, then you go first.

2. The attacker rolls 2D6. If the result is lower than or equal to their *Accuracy*, they have hit the combatant.

3. Subtract the attacker's damage from the defender's *Health*.

4. If the defender has 0 or less *Health*, they have died. If you were the defender, you have died, and you must start the book again.

5. If the defender has 1 or more *Health*, it is their turn to attack.

There is no evade ability, unless mentioned in the paragraph.

If you find a gun in your travels, you can choose to use it in combat. Roll 1D6 to fire the gun instead of attacking, and incur the following damage:

- 1 = Miss
- 2-5 = 2-5 damage
- 6 = Outright kill

The gun will hold 6 bullets and cannot be reloaded during combat. Bullets are not recoverable.

Equipment & Weight

As well as your weapons, you also have a small backpack, which can carry up to 30 weight points.

1. The total weight of all objects carried cannot exceed 30. Any object you can pick up will have an associated weight shown in bold in brackets after the name of the item.

2. If the combined weight of items carried goes over 10, your *Speed* and *Stealth* are reduced by 1 point until the weight falls to 10 or under.

3. If the combined weight of items carried goes over 20, your *Speed* and *Stealth* totals are reduced by a further 1 point until the weight falls to 20 or under.

4. If not in combat, nor about to enter combat, you can discard items to bring the weight carried down. You cannot pick discarded items back up.

5. Your weapons and rations do not count toward your weight limit.

Rations

You start the adventure with 1 ration. Rations, when eaten, restore 5 to your *Health*, though you cannot eat rations mid-combat, or just before entering combat.

Keep a note of how many rations you have using the space on the investigation sheet.

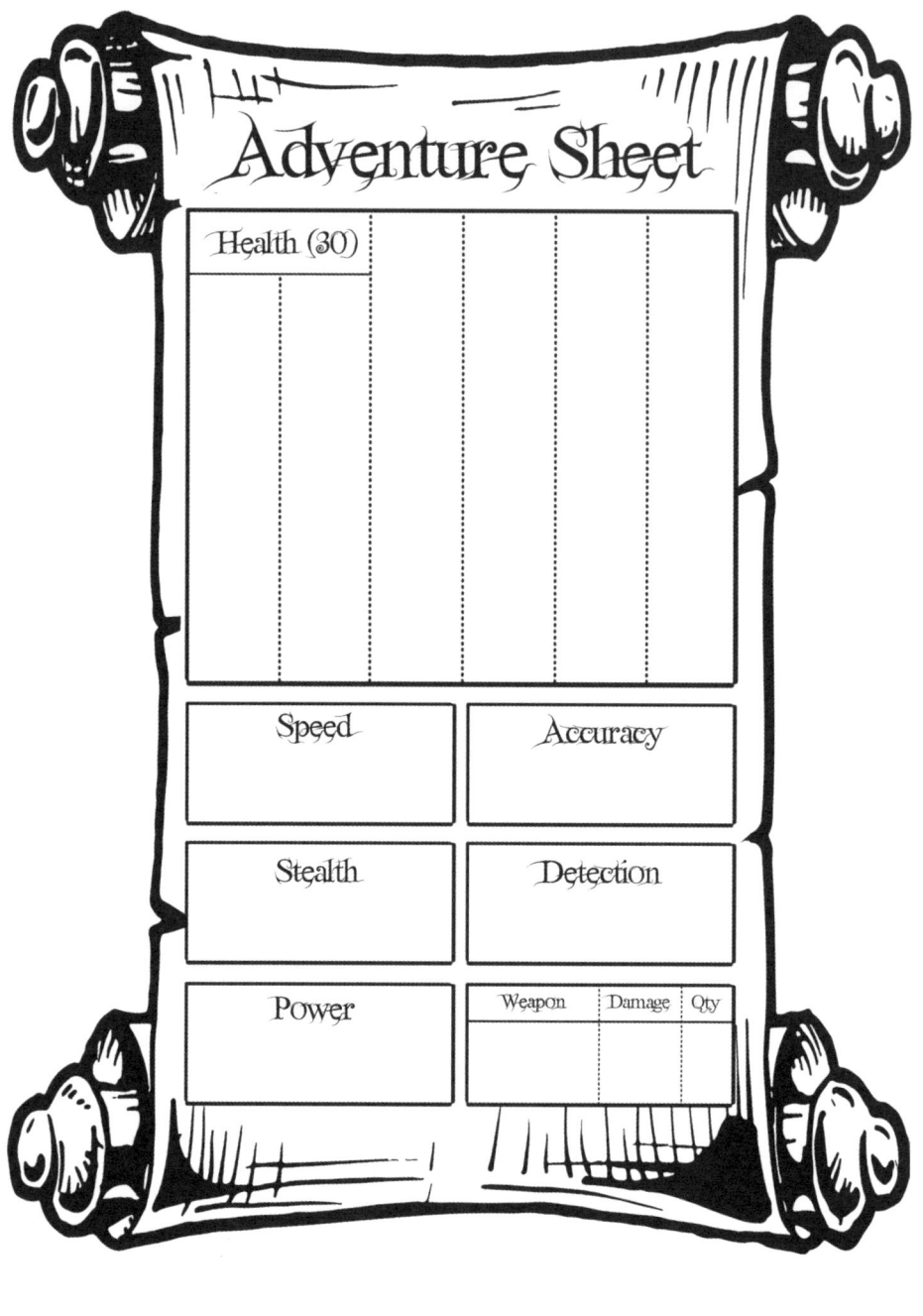

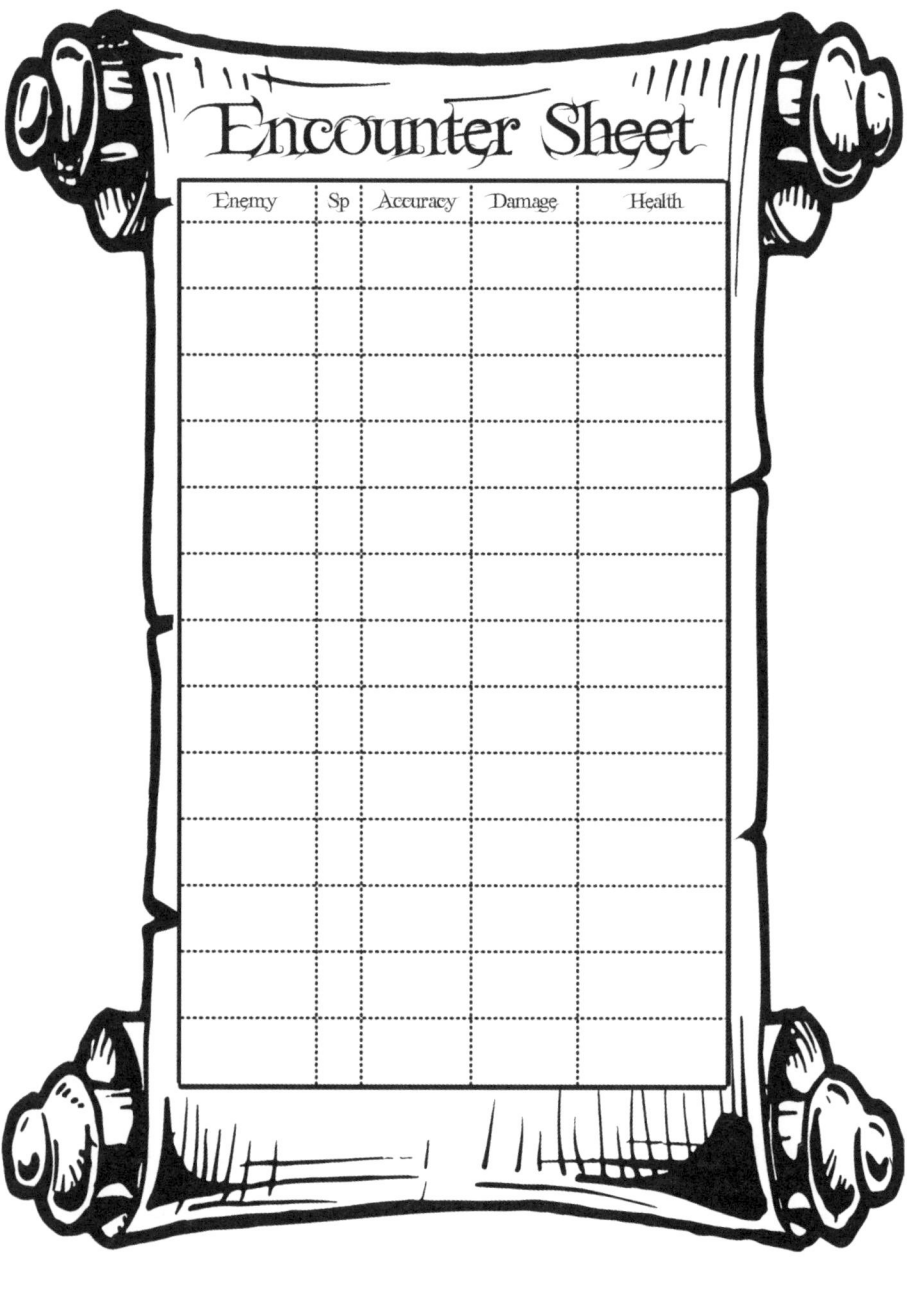

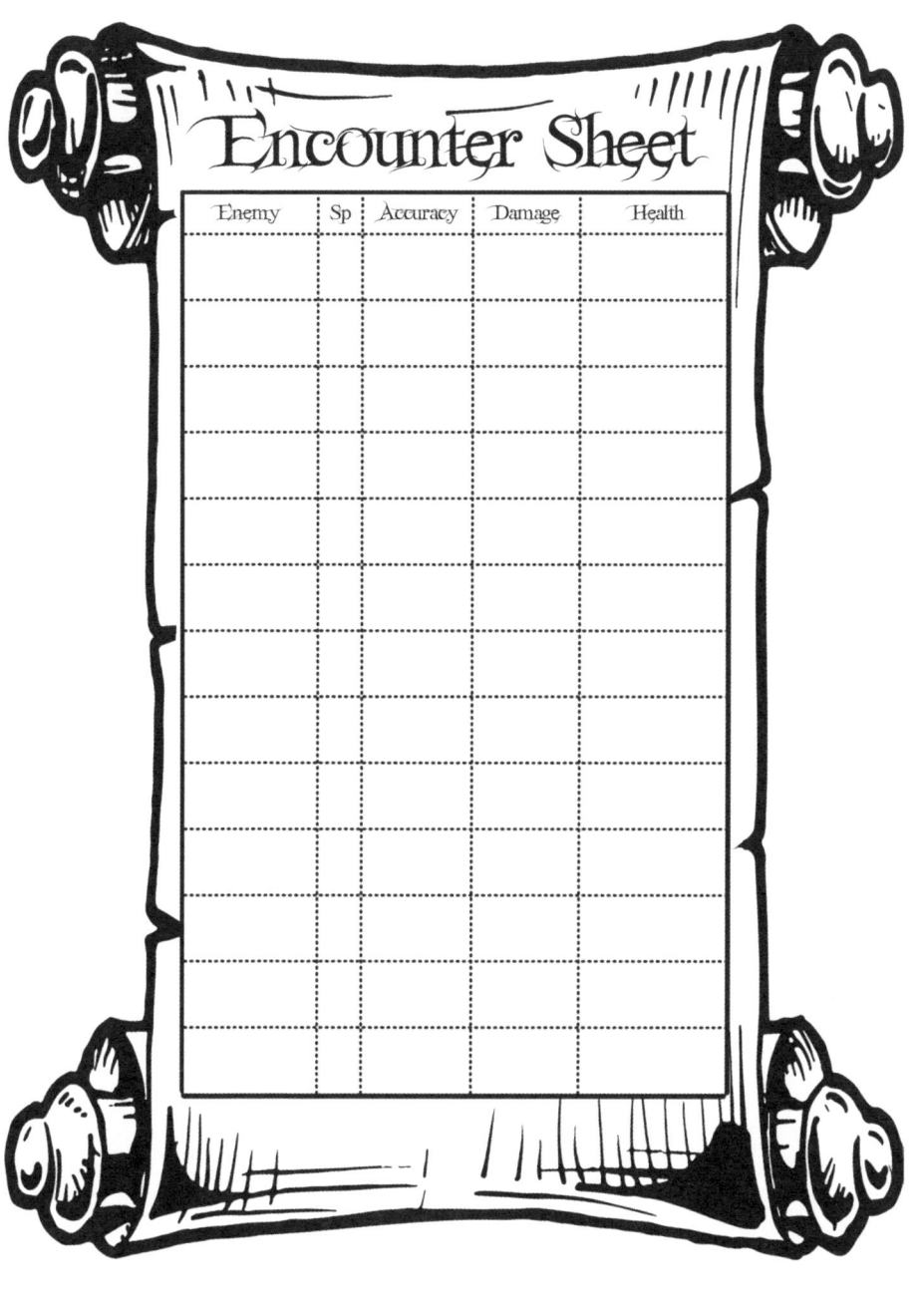

Adventure 01: The Watchtower

Simon Birks

The Watchtower

Welcome to the additional rules for The Watchtower.

These rules should be used in conjunction with the 'General Rules for Adventure' and will take precedence should there be a conflict between the two.

Additional Rules

In 'The Watchtower' you play an adventurer who must infiltrate and takeover a stronghold to allow the advancement of your fellow soldiers.

Your normal weapon is a short sword, with a weapon damage of 1, but you also have a blow pipe with 3 poison darts. Instructions within the sections will tell you how to use the blowpipe in any given situation.

You also have 3 poisoned daggers. Once again, instructions within the sections will tell you how to use the daggers in any given situation.

If you are particularly stealthy, you may also be able to get in a surprise attack before an enemy has time to react.

The section will tell you if you are able to use a *Surprise Attack*. If you can, follow the instructions below:

1. Roll 2D6. If the result is lower than or equal to your *Accuracy*, you have successfully hit the enemy with your normal weapon (initially the short sword).

2. Subtract your weapon's weapon damage from the defender's *Health*.

3. Combat then begins as normal.

A Branching Narrative: The Watchtower

1

The tower is high, though it looked higher before you scaled the rockface which supports it. You are the advance raider – sent to infiltrate and capture this strategic position, so your colleagues can pass safely through the gate below unnoticed. You have been chosen for your skills, and you must not fail.

It's a difficult task but armed as you are with poison darts and poison tipped daggers, you have a fair chance of success.

You afford yourself a moment to wonder what you are doing. It's possible, likely even, that this is a one-way mission, but you know what to do in these times of doubt; you think of your friend and of their fate. The anger builds inside, and you let it. You are here to avenge them.

You don't know how many guards are in the tower, but a count of the windows indicates there'll be three floors and the battlement outside to navigate. You will have to use your experience and cunning to overcome the obstacles before you.

You move into the shadows and wait. You can see the tower door, but it appears shut tight, and is the other side of a largish clearing.

Would you like to inspect the door (**24**), wait where you are (**127**) or scout the area (**49**)?

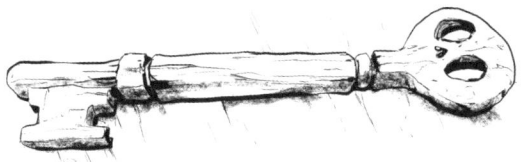

2

The dart misses the guard but alerts them to your presence.

Roll 2d6 and test for *Speed*.

If the test is successful, turn to **130**. Otherwise, turn to **9**.

3

You move to the side, but not quick enough the arrow hits your shoulder.

Deduct 1 from *Power*, *Speed*, *Accuracy* and *Stealth*.

Deduct 3 from *Health*.

Enraged, you swing your sword, and it connects with their left knee, causing them to topple off the steps onto the floor below. They land on their hand with a sickening crunch which tells you they're dead.

Turn to **78**.

4

The Tower Guard doesn't look very happy. You must fight them.

	Speed	*Accuracy*	*Damage*	*Health*
Tower Guard	7	8	2	13

If you defeat the Tower Guard, turn to **14**.

5

At the last minute you realise you're being compelled to drink the liquid and you manage to put the cup back where it was.

You decide to move on quickly - you can head right (**92**) or left (**36**).

6

You reach in and lift the floorboard, which offers no resistance. Putting your hand inside you see a small pouch of purple powder (**+1w**). You've seen something similar before but can't remember where.

You can't see anything else, so decide to look elsewhere (**168**).

7

You look around, trying to work out how you could lure one of them down. You can always wait and see what happens or make a noise and see if they react. Otherwise, you can search the room.

Wait and see	Turn to **77**
Make a noise	Turn to **140**
Examine the bed on the right	Turn to **118**
Examine the bed on the left	Turn to **143**
Investigate the desk	Turn to **67**
Search the guard	Turn to **31**

8

Something about the Widthen's weight feels off. You look at closely and realise it's made of porcelain. Unsure who would have created a fake Widthen (**+3w**), you think about your next move.

Examine the cabinet	Turn to **148**
Head towards the stairs	Turn to **123**

9

You try and scramble up onto the roof, but something gets stuck. You watch, quite helpless, as the guard unsheathes their sword and plunges it into your chest.

Your mission ends here.

10

It's not going to be easy to hide behind the chest.

Roll 2d6 and test for *Stealth*.

If the test is successful, turn to **90**. Otherwise, turn to **79**.

11

You ready your dart and wait. The door opens and before the guard has time to notice you're there, you've fired and hit him in the face.

He croaks something inaudible, then falls to the ground dead.

Emboldened to finish your mission, you head outside (**62**).

12

You pull yourself up onto the roof. Unseen from below, there's a little flat area up there, where a guard is waiting with his sword drawn.

Roll 2d6 and test your *Speed*.

If the test is successful, turn to **37**. Otherwise, turn to **146**.

13

You run up the stairs as quickly as possible. At the top you see the archer is ready.

Roll 2d6 and test for *Speed*.

If the test is successful, turn to **104**. Otherwise, turn to **3**.

14

The Tower Guard falls to the ground safe. Keeping an eye out for other guards, you search his body and find a key (**+2w**), probably for the Tower Door.

Conscious of time, you are caught between trying the key in the door, (turn to **175**) or searching further (turn to **160**).

15

You deftly step behind the guard and slit their throat from behind. They fall to the floor, dead.

Emboldened to complete your mission, you head outside (**62**).

16

You try and get up the stairs quickly, but you're not fast enough.

"Intruder, intruder!" the guard shouts.

In a matter of seconds four guards appear from the higher floors, easily outnumbering you. It doesn't take them long to deal with you.

17

You grab the blanket from the left-hand bed, ball it up and throw it to the mid-way point on the stairs.

An arrow thuds into it from above.

You have little choice but to run up the stairs before the archer has time to ready another shot (**13**).

18

You add the poison to cup Q. Just as you do so you hear footsteps on the battlements outside the door. Looking for a place to hide, you see a chest (**10**) and tiny doorway through to the privy (**88**).

19

You keep to the shadows as best you can and manage to investigate the area. As you turn to head towards the door, you see a flash of metal out of the corner of your eye.

Roll 2d6 and test for *Speed*.

If the test is successful, turn to **147**. Otherwise, turn to **85**.

20

The guard descends to the lowest level, and you let them, knowing they'd have the advantage if they were higher than you.

Are you wearing a pendant?

If so, turn to **177**. Otherwise, turn to **136**.

21

You jump into the bed and pull the covers over you, making sure you can still see out into the room. The guard descends the stairs and scans the room.

Roll 2d6 and test for *Stealth*.

If the test is successful, turn to **131**. Otherwise, turn to **38**.

22

Before you know what you're doing you're drinking the liquid, and you feel it burning all the way down your throat as the acid melts your windpipe. You fall to the ground unable to breathe.

Your mission ends here.

23

Carefully, you're able to navigate the floor before they realise you're there.

They turn at the last minute to face you, obviously scared.

Speak to them	Turn to **42**
Run them through with your sword	Turn to **124**

24

The door is locked and doesn't budge when you apply a little pressure. You don't like being out in the open, so must choose what to do next.

Try to force the door	Turn to **48**
Try to detect a better way in	Turn to **71**
Scout the area	Turn to **49**

25

As you listen, you're sure you hear a bow being pulled back. If so, any attempt to go up the stairs may result in an arrow.

You look around for something to use as cover or a distraction.

Use the body of the old Guard as cover	Turn to **91**
Use a blanket from a bed as a distraction	Turn to **17**
Run up the stairs	Turn to **41**

26

You add the poison to cup J. Just as you do so you hear footsteps on the battlements outside the door. Looking for a place to hide, you see a chest (**10**) and tiny doorway through to the privy (**88**).

27

You add the poison to cup P. Just as you do so you hear footsteps on the battlements outside the door. Looking for a place to hide, you see a chest (**10**) and tiny doorway through to the privy (**88**).

28

You reply and wait a moment. Finally, you hear the person 'grmph' an acceptance.

Turn to **138**.

29

You load up a dart and fire it unhindered. Your skill ensures the darts success, and it lodges in the neck of the guard, who falls from the chair, dead.

Turn to **63**.

30

You walk over to the chest, listening for any movement outside. The chest is unlocked and contains clean uniforms for the guards. A sack you didn't see earlier beside the chest likely contains their dirty clothes.

Suddenly, you hear footsteps on the battlements outside the door. Looking for a place to hide, you decide behind the chest (**10**) or through a tiny doorway which probably leads to the privy (**88**).

31

You move over to the guard and search him. He has a wooden pipe (**+1w**) in his top pocket and pendant (**+1w**) around his neck held on by string. The pendant is made from a common silver coloured metal.

You can try on the pendant (**122**) or look elsewhere (**168**).

32

A quick search of the body recovers a letter sealed with wax which you take. There's no time to look at it, and you're aware the fight may have attracted attention from the guards above.

Run up the stairs	Turn to **41**
Head up the stairs using *Stealth*	Turn to **87**
Wait and listen for movement	Turn to **114**

33

You open the drawer and see a small set of keys (**+2w**), several wicks (**+1w**) and 2 candles (**+1w each**).

Open the cupboard	Turn to **40**
Look at the book	Turn to **141**
Head towards the stairs	Turn to **123**

34

The door opens and a guard enters, not noticing you.

Roll 2d6 and test your *Speed*.

Roll 2d6 and test your *Accuracy*.

Roll 2d6 and test your *Stealth*.

If all three tests are successful, turn to **15**. Otherwise, turn to **156**.

35

You put everything you have into pushing the door open. As you do so, you hear a click, and a cloud of blue gas is shot through a hole in the door you hadn't noticed.

Instantly, you throat closes, and you are unable to breathe. You fall to the floor, writhing, and are only vaguely aware of a tower guard unsheathing his sword before he runs you through with it.

Your adventure ends here.

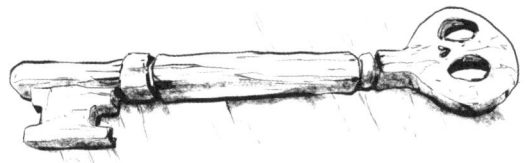

36

After a few steps you stop and listen, trying to pick up on any sound.

You're about to move on when you hear a sound from above. It sounds like there's a guard up there.

You must continue. Do you wish to head right (**66**) or left (**80**)?

37

You drop down towards the tower below, but the guard's blade catches your shoulder.

Deduct 2 from your *Health*.

Roll 2d6 and test for *Accuracy*.

If the test is successful, turn to **172**. Otherwise, turn to **54**.

38

The guard sees you under the covers and immediately walks towards you.

You try and get out but are caught in the sheets. You feel the cold of their sword as they pierce your chest.

You have failed.

39

The dart misses and they are alerted to your presence. You hear a sword being drawn.

You must get up there quickly and deal with them.

Roll 2d6 and test your *Speed*.

If the test is successful, turn to **105**. Otherwise, turn to **16**.

40

You bend down to the cupboard. As you do, the cupboard bursts open and a creature around two feet tall bursts out. The best description you can think of is an upright cat, with a rat's head, and two pairs of muscular arms within which it holds a dagger apiece.

Deduct 1 from your *Health*.

It doesn't look friendly, and starts to circle you slowly, jabbing its daggers as it moves.

You can fight the creature (**76**) or wait and see what it does (**110**).

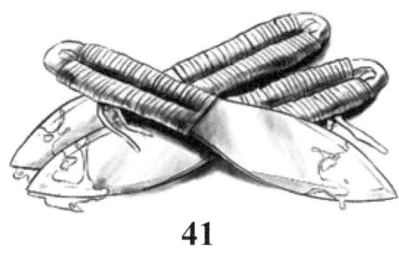

41

If anyone's there you might be able to catch them off guard.

Roll 2d6 and test for *Speed*.

If the test is successful, turn to **99**. Otherwise, turn to **55**.

42

You open your mouth to speak to them, and immediately the guard shouts.

"Intruder, intruder!"

In a matter of seconds four guards appear from the higher floors, easily outnumbering you. It doesn't take them long to deal with you.

43

You launch one of your daggers, unhindered. Your skill ensures the dagger's success, and it lodges in the back of the guard, who falls from the chair, dead.

Turn to **63**.

44

Just as you do so you hear footsteps on the battlements outside the door. Someone's coming in!

Looking for a place to hide, you see a chest (**10**) and tiny doorway through to the privy (**88**).

45

The guard calls for help. Without warning, the window opens, and a spear is forced through your neck.

Your mission ends here.

46

You start to take the stairs slowly, one step at a time.

Roll 2d6 and test for *Detection*.

If you are successful, turn to **151**. Otherwise, turn to **154**.

47

You keep to the shadows successfully and manage to investigate the area. Unfortunately, you find nothing, but just as you're about to head to the door, you hear a noise, and decide to investigate (turn to **64**).

48

You put your shoulder against the door and dig your feet into the ground.

Roll 2d6 and test for *Power*.

If the test is successful, turn to **35**. Otherwise, turn to **96**.

49

Keeping to the shadows you move around the vicinity immediately adjacent to the tower.

Roll 2d6 and test your *Stealth*.

If the test is successful, turn to **47**. Otherwise, turn to **19**.

50

You begin to open the hatch, hoping you're making as little noise as possible. You see a guard with their back to you looking over the edge. You open the hatch fully without making a sound.

You have two choices; fire a dart if you have one (**145**) or creep up onto the roof (**52**).

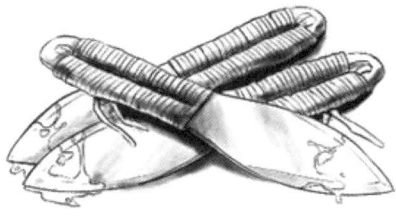

51

You quickly search the nearby area but find nothing. Not wanting to waste any more time, you go to the Tower door to try the key (**175**).

52

You carefully make your way onto the roof. At the last moment, the guard turns around and is surprised to see you.

Make 1 Surprise Attack against the guard.

If the surprise attack is successful, remember to deduct your weapon damage from the *Health* shown below.

	Speed	*Accuracy*	*Damage*	*Health*
Guard	11	10	3	15

If you win, turn to **173**.

53

Your observations confirm what you thought, the door is boobytrapped and an attempt to force it would trigger a poison to be emitted through a small hole in the door at eye level.

You take a step back to work out what you should do next, and as you do so, you see a Tower Guard approaching.

You must deal with him somehow before it's safe to enter the tower.

You have an excellent opportunity to use a dart or a dagger if you wish.

Alternatively, you can attack him.

Shoot a dart at him	Turn to **164**
Throw a dagger at him	Turn to **169**
Fight the Tower Guard	Turn to **4**

54

You land on the railing, seriously injuring your back.

Reduce your *Stealth* by 2.

Reduce your *Accuracy* by 1.

Reduce your *Speed* by 1.

Deduct 2 from your *Health*.

If you're still alive, you can go left (turn to **92**) or right (turn to **80**) around the tower.

55

You attempt to run up the stairs, but stumble slightly. You feel an arrow graze your side.

Deduct 2 from your *Health*.

You make it to the second floor and grab the archer's bow and haul him down from the steps.

Without the bow, the archer is armed only with a knife.

	Speed	*Accuracy*	*Damage*	*Health*
Archer	8	6	1	8

If you win, turn to **78**.

56

The dart embeds into the guard's neck. During your fight with him, deduct 2 from his *Health* at the end of each round for poison damage. Turn to **4**.

57

You bite down into the fruit, which turns out to be fake and made of porcelain.

Deduct 1 from your *Health*.

It drops onto your foot and rolls away into the darkness.

Confused and wondering why there should be fake fruit on the table, you can now either head towards the stairs (turn to **123**) or examine the cabinet (turn to **148**).

58

The liquid has a shimmering quality about it, and you're almost unaware that you have picked the cup up.

Roll 2d6 and test for *Detection*.

If the test is successful, turn to **5**. Otherwise, turn to **22**.

59

You jump into the bed and pull the covers over you, making sure you can still see out into the room. The guard descends the stairs and scans the room.

Roll 2d6 and test for *Stealth*.

If the test is successful, turn to **131**. Otherwise, turn to **38**.

60

You jump out of bed and bring your sword down on the back of the guard, inflicting some damage. They turn to fight you.

	Speed	Accuracy	Damage	Health
Guard	7	8	2	9

If you win, turn to **32**.

61

The dart hits the guard, and they grunt once before falling to the floor. You scramble up onto the roof to make sure they are dead. They are.

Now, turn to **173**.

62

You step outside, unsure how many guards are here. You can see the forest below, where your colleagues wait for the all-clear signal.

The small gangway you're now standing on runs the circumference of the tower. You can't see or hear anyone else at the moment, but they must be close.

You could possibly stand on the railing and pull yourself onto the sloping roof. Other than that, you can either head left, or right?

Head left around the tower	Turn to **92**
Head right around the tower	Turn to **80**
Try and get onto the roof	Turn to **84**

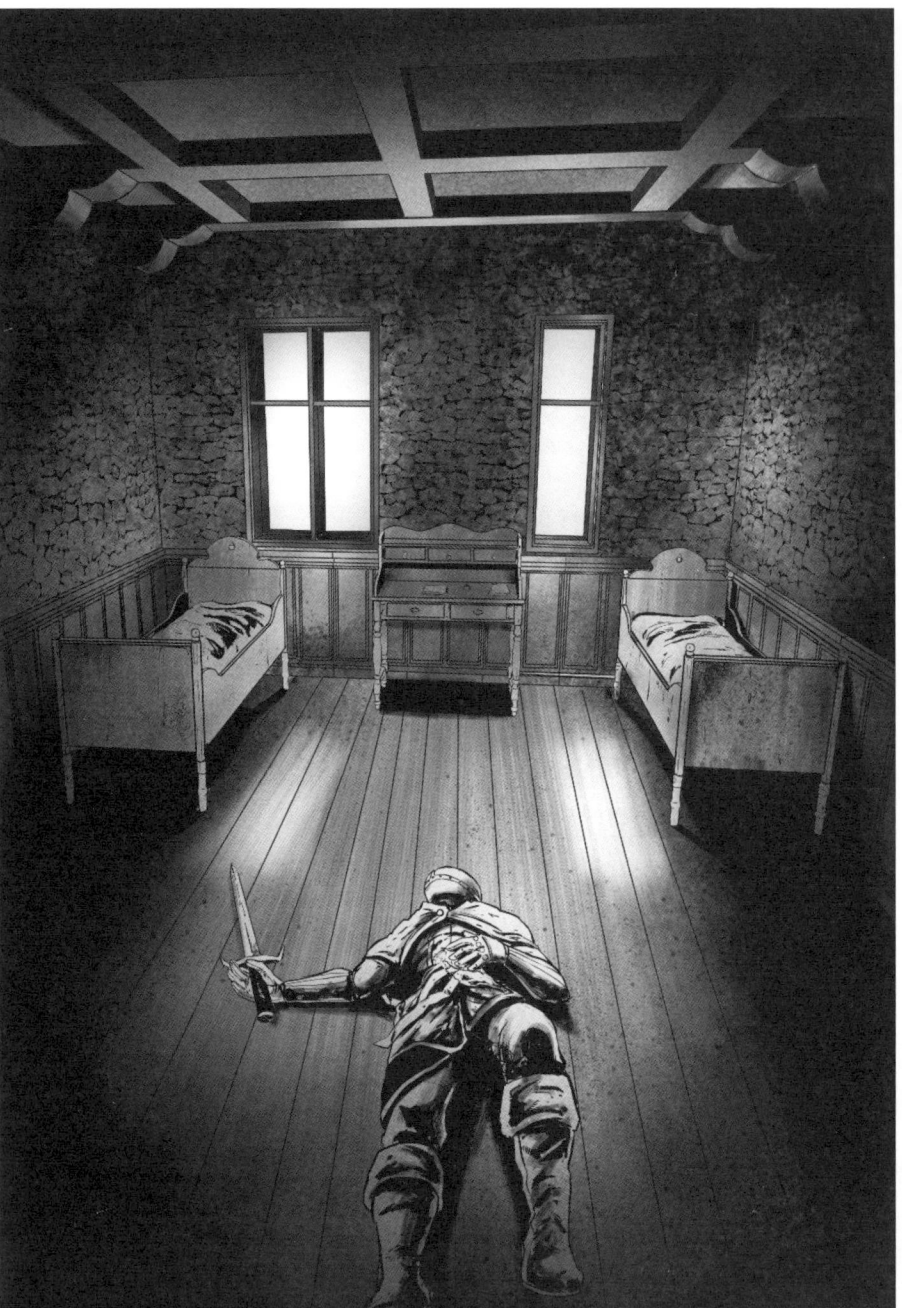

63

The body of the guard lies on the floor. This room houses two beds on opposite sides, as well as a desk. A window looks out above the desk where you know your fellow soldiers are waiting to be alerted of your success.

You shouldn't keep them waiting.

What would you like to do?

Continue up to the next floor	Turn to **75**
Examine the bed on the left	Turn to **143**
Look at the bed on the right	Turn to **118**
Investigate the desk	Turn to **67**
Search the guard	Turn to **31**

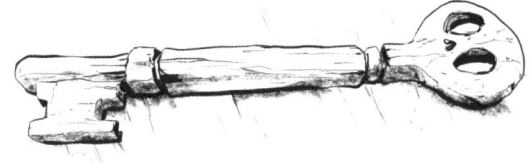

64

You move slowly toward the direction of the noise, and after taking only two steps you see a Tower Guard with his back to you. It takes you a couple of seconds to realise he's urinating into the foliage on the other side of the path.

You must deal with him somehow before it's safe to enter the tower.

You have an excellent opportunity to use a dart or a dagger if you wish.

Alternatively, you can attack him.

Throw a dagger at him	Turn to **169**
Shoot a dart at him	Turn to **164**
Attack him with your sword	Turn to **4**

65

You begin to open the hatch, hoping you're making as little noise as possible. You see a guard with their back to you looking over the edge. Just as you're thinking you might be able to surprise them, the hatch squeaks and the guard turns around.

Roll 2d6 and test your *Speed*.

If the test is successful, turn to **130**. Otherwise, turn to **9**.

66

You keep moving, and soon notice a small altar shaped into the wall. By the altar is cup of purple liquid. It doesn't smell of anything.

Continue left around the wall	Turn to **36**
Head back right	Turn to **92**
Taste the liquid	Turn to **58**

67

Open on the desk is a journal that the guard must have been writing in just before his death. You read the first page.

"I have the powder now, and it's just a matter of time. At first, I thought I would use it on Jurita, and get rid of the idiot once and for all, but now my mind turns to a more personal use. They say the poison is sweet and you cannot find a better way to die. Maybe this would be a welcome relief, especially at my stage of life... Piotr"

All the other drawers are locked.

Slightly saddened at reading the journal, you decide to look elsewhere in the room (**168**).

68

Quietly, you climb the ladder and stop at the hatch. You can't hear anything beyond, but know you'd be at a disadvantage if someone was up there.

Roll 2d6 and test for *Stealth*.

If the test is successful, turn to **50**. Otherwise, turn to **65**.

69

You pick up the Widthen, which feels cool to your touch.

Roll 2d6 and test for *Detection*.

If the test is successful, turn to **8**. Otherwise, turn to **57**.

70

You look over the table, but nothing seems out of place. The fruit look tempting, and you can try one of them if you'd like to regain any strength.

Try one of the fruits	Turn to **144**
Examine the cabinet	Turn to **112**
Head towards the stairs	Turn to **123**

71

You look around the doorframe, trying to see if you can open the door without forcing it.

Roll 2d6 and test for *Detection*.

If the test is successful, turn to **53**. Otherwise, turn to **152**.

72

The guard gasps and you realise you've been spotted.

You turn as they draw their sword. You must fight now.

	Speed	Accuracy	Damage	Health
Guard	9	8	2	11

If you win, turn to **171**.

73

Slowly, you move up the stairs, trying to be as silent as possible.

Unfortunately, you see the archer too late, and arrow they unleash hits you square in the eye.

Your mission ends here.

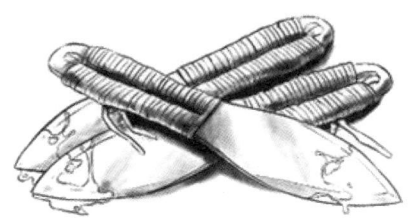

74

Each of the bowls has a letter on it. J, P, W and Q. Which one would you like to poison?

Poison J	Turn to **26**
Poison P	Turn to **27**
Poison W	Turn to **107**
Poison Q	Turn to **18**

75

You carefully approach the stairs and listen. At the top you can hear a discussion between three different people about what they want for dinner. They sound younger than the guard you dispatched on this floor, and it's unlikely you would come off best against so many of them.

Try and get one of the guards to come down	Turn to **7**
Examine the bed on the left	Turn to **143**
Examine the bed on the right	Turn to **118**
Investigate the desk	Turn to **67**
Search the guard	Turn to **31**

76

You draw your weapon and approach the creature. It's fast and can get in two attacks for your one.

	Speed	Accuracy	Damage	Health
CatRat	10	7	1	8

If you win, turn to **165**.

77

You wait a little while, listening. Surely, they can't talk about food all night. Fortunately, they don't and after a minute or so, they conclude their discussions, and you hear them moving off. It sounds like two of them go upstairs to the higher floors, leaving one in the room above.

Creep up the stairs	Turn to **46**
Examine the bed on the left	Turn to **143**
Search the guard	Turn to **31**
Look at the bed on the right	Turn to **118**
Investigate the desk	Turn to **67**

78

This appears to be the final floor of the tower, as opposite you is a door leading out onto the battlements. There are weapons mounted onto the wall, including a sturdy looking shield (**+4w**) and a mace (**+4w**). The shield will give you extra shielding and will block a successful attack against you on a roll of 5-6 on a 1d6, and the mace has a weapon damage of 3.

If you'd like to take them, make a note on your adventure sheet.

You notice there are four cups of broth on the table in the centre, none of them drunk from, alongside a dog-eared deck of cards (**+1w**).

There is a shuttered window off to your right, and a large chest near the other door.

If you have some purple powder	Turn to **89**
Listen at the door	Turn to **44**
Go through the door	Turn to **170**
Investigate the window	Turn to **132**
Investigate the chest	Turn to **30**

79

The guard gasps and you realise you've been spotted.

You jump up as they draw their sword. You must fight now.

	Speed	Accuracy	Damage	Health
Guard	9	8	2	11

If you win, turn to **171**.

80

As you keep moving, you begin to feel uneasy, but you aren't sure why.

Suddenly, something shoots out from the darkness where the rood meets the wall.

Roll 2d6 and test for *Speed*.

If the test is successful, turn to **121**. Otherwise, turn to **157**.

81

You muster all your power and jump into the room. Unhindered by any obstacle you overbalance and fall into the table in the centre of the room, knocking a bowl of fruit off and onto the floor, where you hear a something smash like a cup. You check the floor and see one of the fruits was fake and contained a sapphire (**+2w**) which winks at you from the floor.

There is a set of stairs on one wall, and cabinet on the other.

Head towards the stairs	Turn to **123**
Examine the cabinet	Turn to **148**

82

The body of the old man crashes into the archer knocking him from the stairs. He lands on his head with a sickening crunch. You don't need to inspect him to know he's dead.

Now, turn to **78**.

83

Nervous at being found out, you prepare one of your darts and creep to a position where you can see part of the person.

Roll 2d6 and test for *Accuracy*.

If the test is successful, turn to **116**. Otherwise, turn to **39**.

84

You get onto the railing and attempt to pull yourself up onto the roof.

Roll 2d6 and test for *Power*.

If the test is successful, turn to **12**. Otherwise, turn to **125**.

85

You move as quickly as you can, but the blade still connects with you.

Deduct 4 from your *Health*.

There's no time for darts or daggers. You must face your opponent.

Turn to **4**.

86

Unsurprisingly, it misses and hits the wall harmlessly. At least it throws the archer out of their stride a little.

You have little choice but run up the stairs (turn to **13**).

87

Perhaps if you crept up the stairs no-one would hear you.

Roll 2d6 and test for *Stealth*.

If the test is successful, turn to **73**. Otherwise, turn to **113**.

88

You'll need to be quick to get over there.

Roll 2d6 and test for *Speed*.

If the test is successful, turn to **108**. Otherwise, turn to **72**.

89

You realise it might be possible to poison one of the Guards. Otherwise, you can search the room or go through the door.

Poison one of the cups	Turn to **74**
Listen at the door	Turn to **44**
Go through the door	Turn to **170**
Investigate the window	Turn to **132**
Investigate the chest	Turn to **30**

90

You duck down behind the chest and wait. It's a squeeze, but you're confident they won't see you. The door opens and you hear footsteps crossing the floor. They pick up bowls from the table and then you hear them walk out. Relieved you head back into the room.

If you poisoned bowl J or W	Turn to **167**
If you poisoned bowl Q or P	Turn to **117**
If you didn't poison any bowl	Turn to **120**

91

You attempt to lift the old Guard up.

Roll 2d6 and test for *Power*.

If the test is successful, turn to **153**. Otherwise, turn to **103**.

92

You walk around the tower and see a ladder leading up to a trapdoor which must lead onto the roof.

Continue left	Turn to **66**
Head up to the roof	Turn to **68**
Head back right	Turn to **155**

93

The dagger finds its target and the archer falls from the steps, hitting their head with a sickening crunch on the floor. You don't need to inspect the body to know its dead.

You make your way all the way up to the second floor (turn to **78**).

94

You have time to ready a dart or dagger if you have one.

Ready a dart	Turn to **11**
Ready a dagger	Turn to **163**
Do neither	Turn to **149**

95

The dart finds its target and the archer falls before they have a chance to fire another arrow. As you run up the stairs you see them fall off the steps and land with a sickening crunch on their head. They're most definitely dead.

Turn to **78**.

96

You put everything you have into pushing the door open. No matter how hard you push, the door doesn't budge, and as you attempt to try harder, you notice a tiny hole in the door which you realise is a boobytrap. You drop to the floor as a jet of blue gas shoots harmlessly over your head.

No sooner have you thanked the gods, than a Tower Guard approaches, sword drawn, ready to fight.

Turn to **4**.

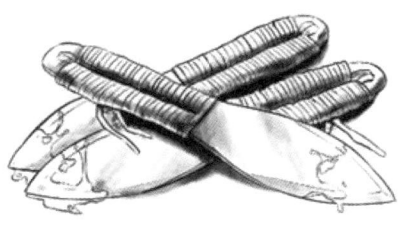

97

You reply and instantly hear the guard's concern. You hear them unsheathing their sword.

You must get up the stairs as quickly as possible.

Roll 2d6 and test for *Speed*.

If the test is successful, turn to **105**. Otherwise, turn to **16**.

98

You throw it quickly.

Roll 2d6 and test for *Accuracy*.

Roll 2d6 and test for *Power*.

If both tests are successful, turn to **134**. Otherwise, turn to **45**.

99

You sprint up the stairs with surprising grace. You hear an arrow hit the wall behind you and before their have time to prepare another you are near them.

You swing your sword with everything you have, catching the archer's knee. They buckle and fall from the steps, landing on their head with a sickening crunch. They won't be getting up again.

Now, turn to **78**.

100

You manage to navigate the stairs efficiently to not make a noise.

Sitting a little away with their back to you is a guard.

Get closer to the guard	Turn to **23**
Use a poison dart (if you have one)	Turn to **29**
Use a poisoned dagger (if you have one)	Turn to **43**

101

You pull back the covers to reveal a sheathed sword. You pick it up and inspect it. It's a fine sword, better than your current weapon, though a little heavier. If you wish to take it add **+1w** and increase your weapon damage to 3.

Now, turn to **168**.

102

The dart misses the target and embeds itself in a nearby tree.

You must now fight the guard.

Turn to **4**.

103

Try as you might, you cannot lift the old guard. What would you like to do, now?

Use a blanket from the bed as a distraction	Turn to **17**
Run up the stairs	Turn to **13**

104

You roll out of the way and the arrow strikes the wall where you were standing.

In one deft move, your sword finds the archer's left knee, and they buckle and fall from the steps, landing heavily on their head as they hit the floor. The sickening crunch tells you they are dead.

Now, turn to **78**.

105

You are up the stairs in a couple of seconds. The opponent in front of you is older, and they cower as you approach.

Speak to them — Turn to **42**
Run them through with your sword — Turn to **124**

106

The dagger lands firmly in the guards back. Turn to **4** to fight the Tower Guard but reduce his starting *Health* by 3. During your fight with him, deduct 1 from his *Health* at the end of each round for poison damage.

107

You add the poison to cup W. Just as you do so you hear footsteps on the battlements outside the door. Looking for a place to hide, you see a chest (**10**) and a tiny doorway through to the privy (**88**).

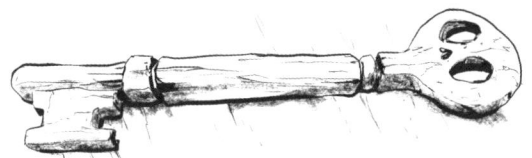

108

You make it to the doorway and duck in just in time.

The door opens and you hear footsteps crossing the floor. They pick up bowls from the table and then you hear them walk out.

Relieved you head back into the room.

If you poisoned bowl J or W — Turn to **167**
If you poisoned bowl Q or P — Turn to **117**
If you didn't poison any bowl — Turn to **120**

109

No sooner have you started your ascent than you step on a squeaky stair. You hear movement and see a guard come into view.

You must get up the stairs quickly.

Roll 2d6 and test for *Speed*.

If the test is successful, turn to **105**. Otherwise, turn to **16**.

110

Whilst it continues to circle you in a threatening manner it doesn't get any closer. You realise it's heading towards the door and step back to let it leave.

It runs out into the night without looking back.

You investigate the cupboard it came from and notice a rope which has been gnawed in two. Perhaps this creature was a prisoner here. You'll never know.

There are noises overhead, so you decide to waste no time and head to the stairs.

Turn to **123**.

111

You turn and investigate the room once more.

Look at the bed on the right	Turn to **118**
Search the guard	Turn to **31**
Investigate the desk	Turn to **67**

112

You make your way to the cabinet without incident. There's nothing particularly interesting about it. There's a book resting on the top, the drawer, and the cupboard underneath.

You think you hear a noise on the floor above you.

Look at the book	Turn to **141**
Check the drawer	Turn to **33**
Open the cupboard	Turn to **40**
Leave it and head towards the stairs	Turn to **123**

113

As you begin to creep up the stairs, your sword catches on a step forcing you bend down to free it. As you do so an arrow flies past your head.

You quickly think of your options.

Run up the stairs	Turn to **13**
Throw a dagger (if you have one)	Turn to **176**
Use a dart (if you have one)	Turn to **158**

114

You stand still and slow your breathing.

Roll 2d6 and test for *Detection*.

If the test is successful, turn to **25**. Otherwise, turn to **174**

115

The body of the guard hits the archer, knocking their bow out of their hands. They jump down off the stairs.

Without the bow, the archer is armed only with a knife.

	Speed	Accuracy	Damage	Health
Archer	8	6	1	8

If you win, turn to **78**.

116

You blow the dart, and it impales into the person's neck. They fall quickly, dead, and you waste no time moving up the stairs quickly.

Turn to **63**.

117

After a couple of moments, the door is opened and a guard staggers in holding their throat - clearly you chose the right bowl. They fall in front of you, dead.

Emboldened to finish your mission, you head outside (turn to **62**).

118

You approach the bed and notice a definite shape within the covers. It's too flat to be a person.

    Pull back the covers   Turn to **101**
    Look elsewhere   Turn to **168**

119

Not sure what to do, you decide to do nothing. You wait and can hear the person breathing above.

Roll 2d6 and test for *Detection*.

If the test is successful, turn to **133**. Otherwise, turn to **83**.

120

Just as you're thinking about your next move you hear footsteps coming toward the door. You can't reach either previous hiding place in time.

    Stand your ground and fight   Turn to **94**
    Hide behind the door   Turn to **34**

121

You manage to dart just out of the way as something shoots by your head and over the side of the railing. You assume it must be a Vorp, or spitting bug, and you thank the gods it missed you.

Quickly, you must decide to head left (turn to **155**) or right (turn to **36**).

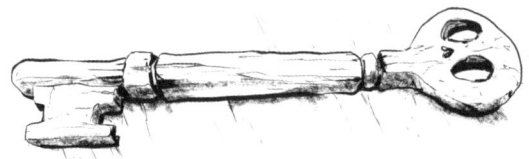

122

You lift the string over your head and let the pendant rest against your skin. Not sure what to expect, you are still underwhelmed when nothing happens.

Now, turn to **168**.

123

As you make your way towards the stairs you hear footsteps above you.

"Is that you, Jurita?" asks a voice.

You're unsure if that's a male or female name.

Answer 'Yes' in a female voice	Turn to **97**
Answer 'Yes' in a male voice	Turn to **28**
Don't reply and stand still	Turn to **119**

124

You have no hesitation in killing them and they quickly fall to the ground dead.

Now, turn to **63**.

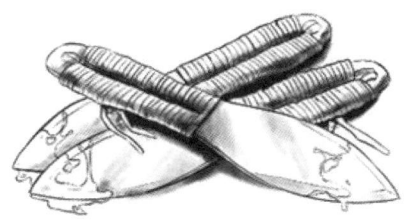

125

Unable to pull yourself up, you can only head left (**92**) or right (**80**) around the tower.

126

You quietly push the door open and look round in the room. The bottom floor isn't well lit, but you can't see anyone obvious. Off to the right a staircase winds upwards against the wall. In the centre of the room a rough table with three chairs sits empty, a basket of fruit in its centre. Further to the right is a small cabinet, with a drawer at the top and a cupboard beneath.

Examine the table — Turn to **70**
Examine the cabinet — Turn to **112**
Head towards the stairs — Turn to **123**

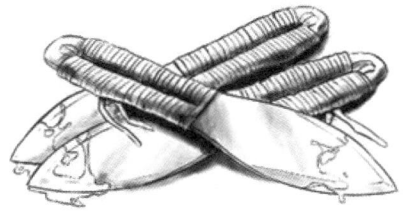

127

You wait, sensing all is too quiet. You think you hear a noise but aren't sure.

Investigate the noise — Turn to **64**
Wait longer — Turn to **142**
Inspect the door — Turn to **24**
Scout the area — Turn to **49**

128

The dagger nicks the guard, but nothing more. Turn to **4** to fight the guard. During your fight with him, deduct 1 from his *Health* at the end of each round for poison damage.

129

You pick up the Dringberry and pop it into your mouth whole. It tastes delicious.

Restore 1 to your *Health*.

Examine the cabinet Turn to **148**
Head towards the stairs Turn to **123**

130

You scramble up onto the roof, parrying the guard's sword. You must fight them.

	Speed	*Accuracy*	*Damage*	*Health*
Guard	11	10	3	15

If you win, turn to **173**.

131

You're hidden well enough that they don't see you, and instead their attention goes to their fallen colleague. Now's your chance for a surprise attack.

Roll 2d6 and test for *Speed*.

If the test is successful, turn to **150**. Otherwise, turn to **60**.

132

You go to the window and listen but hear nothing outside. Suddenly, the outside door opens and a guard walks in. They see you almost immediately, but you may have time to throw a dagger if you have one.

If you still have a dagger, turn to **98**. Otherwise, turn to **45**.

133

You try and work out the best thing to do. As you listen to them breathing, you realise it's more of a wheeze, and assume the person is older and less likely to want to come down the stairs. You decide to wait it out, and after another ten seconds, you hear the person return to a chair.

Now, turn to **138**.

134

The dagger lodges in the guard's neck and they fall to the floor, dead. You go to them and drag them further into the room.

Emboldened to complete your mission, you head outside (turn to **62**).

135

Have you recently found a new weapon?

If so, turn to **21**. Otherwise, turn to **166**.

136

You must fight the guard.

	Speed	Accuracy	Damage	Health
Guard	9	9	2	10

If you win, turn to **32**.

137

You take the Magrijin and peel it, breathing in the sweet aroma. It smells divine, and you quickly devour it.

Restore 2 to your *Health*.

Head towards the stairs	Turn to **123**
Examine the cabinet	Turn to **148**

138

You must creep carefully up the stairs.

Roll 2d6 and test for *Stealth* 3 times.

If all 3 tests are successful, turn to **100**. Otherwise, turn to **109**.

139

You begin to look for another way into the tower but have no sooner started when you hear a noise behind you, and you turn to face a Tower Guard, ready to attack.

Turn to **4**.

140

You move the chair noisily and wait. Nothing happens. You decide to topple the chair over which clatters to the floor. You hear a guard get up and walk over to the stairs. You can find a place to hide or stand your ground.

Stand your ground	Turn to **20**
Hide in the bed on the left	Turn to **59**
Hide in the bed on the right	Turn to **135**

141

The light isn't good by the cupboard, so you take the book into the centre of the room to look at it closer. As you do, the cupboard bursts open and a creature around two feet tall bursts out. The best description you can think of is an upright cat, with a rat's head, and two pairs of muscular arms within which it holds a dagger apiece.

It doesn't look friendly, and starts to circle you slowly, jabbing its daggers as it does so.

Fight the creature	Turn to **76**
Wait and see what it does	Turn to **110**

142

You wait a little longer. Without warning, you see a flash of metal out of the corner of your eye.

Roll 2d6 and test for *Speed*.

If the test is successful, turn to **147**. Otherwise, turn to **85**.

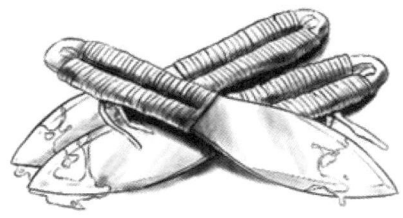

143

You go to the bed and move the covers and look under the mattress. It's not a nice experience and brings you no rewards.

Roll 2d6 and test for *Detection*.

If the test is successful, turn to **159**. Otherwise, turn to **111**.

144

Which would you like to try?

Eat the sweet Dringberry   Turn to **129**
Crunch into the ripe Widthen   Turn to **69**
Peel the fragrant Magrijin   Turn to **137**

145

The light isn't good, but the target isn't too far away.

You ready your dart.

Roll 2d6 and test for *Accuracy*.

If the test is successful, turn to **61**. Otherwise, turn to **2**.

146

You're unable to dodge their blade, and it pierces your heart, killing you instantly. Your mission ends here.

147

You move as quickly as you can, but the blade still connects with you.

Deduct 2 from your *Health*.

There's no time for darts or daggers. You must face your opponent.

Now, turn to **4**.

148

You start to turn towards the cabinet when you hear a scraping chair above. Carefully you step towards the stairs.

Turn to **123**.

149

The guard enters and you engage them immediately in combat. Due to their surprise, you're able to get a Surprise Attack in before they can react.

Whether the Surprise Attack is successful or not (if it is, remember to deduct your weapon damage from the *Health* shown below), you now fight as normal.

	Speed	*Accuracy*	*Damage*	*Health*
Guard	9	8	2	11

If you win, turn to **171**.

150

You jump out of bed and bring your sword down on the back of the guard, inflicting grave damage. They turn to fight you.

	Speed	*Accuracy*	*Damage*	*Health*
Guard	5	6	2	6

If you win, turn to **32**.

151

Fortunately, you notice one of the steps is higher than the others and manage to step over it.

You stop when you can see into the room above. There is one guard preparing food on a central table. You can smell herbs in the air.

Without warning you hear more feet on the stairs to the next level and you retreat down quickly.

Make a noise to attract one of the guards	Turn to **140**
Search the guard	Turn to **31**
Look at the bed on the right	Turn to **118**
Investigate the desk	Turn to **67**
Examine the bed on the left	Turn to **143**

152

Your observations reveal nothing untoward about the door.

Try to force the door	Turn to **48**
Look for another way in	Turn to **139**

153

You lift the guard up and make your way up the stairs. About halfway up you hear the thud of an arrow hitting the old man's body. You press on quickly and before the archer has time to knock another arrow, you're close enough to throw the body.

Roll 2d6 and test for *Accuracy*.

If the test is successful, turn to **82**. Otherwise, turn to **115**.

154

You fail to notice one of the steps has been made deliberately higher than the others to catch intruders out and stumble on it. You manage to jump back to the floor, but hear a guard get up and walk over to the stairs. You can find a place to hide or stand your ground.

Stand your ground	Turn to **20**
Hide in the bed on the right	Turn to **135**
Hide in the bed on the left	Turn to **59**

155

You come to the door you came out of. There's no real reason to go back in.

Head left around the tower	Turn to **92**
Head up to the roof	Turn to **68**
Head right around the tower	Turn to **80**

156

The guard realises you're there and turns to face you weapon drawn.

	Speed	*Accuracy*	*Damage*	*Health*
Guard	9	8	2	11

If you win, turn to **171**.

157

Something embeds itself in your cheek. You pull a small spine out of your flesh, and immediately recognise it as one from a Vorp, or spitting bug.

Deduct 1 from your *Health*.

Quickly, you must head left (**155**) or right (**36**).

158

It's not going to be easy.

Roll 2d6, subtract 1 and test for *Accuracy*.

If the test is successful, turn to **95**. Otherwise, turn to **161**.

159

As you go to put the mattress back down, you notice something strange about the floorboards under the bed.

You get on your knees and look underneath. One of the floorboards is slightly raised.

Would you like to investigate the floorboard (**6**) or look elsewhere (**168**)?

160

You decide to see if you can find anything else.

Roll 2d6 and test for *Detection*.

If the test is successful, turn to **162**. Otherwise, turn to **51**.

161

Not surprisingly, the dart misses, and the archer has enough time to loose another arrow as you head up the stairs. The arrow thuds into your chest, and you feel the life drain out of you.

Your mission ends here.

162

Noticing some dirt on the knees of the guard, you search around the edges of the path and find a patch of newly dug earth. You dig into it, and quickly find a small green metal box (**+1w**). It is jammed shut, and you don't want to take the time to attempt to open it.

Realising you must enter the tower, you go to the door to try the key.

Turn to **175**.

163

You ready your dagger and wait. The door opens and before the guard has time to notice you're there, you've thrown it and hit him in the chest.

He croaks something inaudible, then falls to the ground dead.

Emboldened to finish your mission, you head outside.

Turn to **62**.

164

You load a dart into the pipe, steady yourself and blow.

Roll 2d6 and test for *Accuracy*.

If the test is successful, turn to **56**. Otherwise, turn to **102**.

165

The CatRat lies dead on the floor. You search its body and find nothing. You notice burn marks around its wrists, and when you inspect the cupboard, you notice a rope which has been gnawed in two. Perhaps this creature was a prisoner here. You'll never know.

There are noises overhead, so you decide to waste no time and head to the stairs.

Turn to **123**.

166

You go to hide in the bed but as you pull back the covers something clatters to the ground. It takes you a moment to take it in, but that's enough time for the guard to start coming down the stairs.

Turn to **20**.

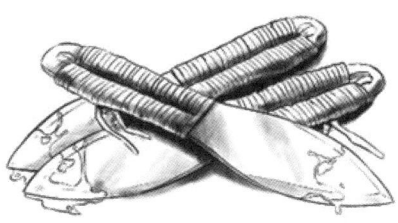

167

You see that your poisoned bowl is still on the table - it must have belonged to one of the guards you already killed.

Just as you're thinking about your next move you hear footsteps coming toward the door. You can't reach either previous hiding place in time.

Stand your ground and fight	Turn to **94**
Hide behind the door	Turn to **34**

168

As you step back into the room, your clumsily knock into the chair which falls to the floor with a great clatter.

You hear the guard get up and walk over to the stairs. You can find a place to hide or stand your ground.

Stand your ground	Turn to **20**
Hide in the bed on the left	Turn to **59**
Hide in the bed on the right	Turn to **135**

169

You fetch one of your knives, steady yourself and throw.

Roll 2d6 and test for *Accuracy*.

If the test is successful, turn to **106**. Otherwise, turn to **128**.

170

Just as you're about to try the door, you hear footsteps on the battlements outside. Someone's coming in!

Looking for a place to hide, you see a chest (**10**) and a tiny doorway through to the privy (**88**).

171

You're pretty sure the other guard will soon be missed, so decide to head outside and finish the mission.

Now, turn to **62**.

172

You land awkwardly on your ankle, but at least you're safe.

Reduce your *Stealth* by 1.

You can now head left (**92**) or right (**80**) around the tower.

173

As your weapon delivers its final blow, the guard falls, and a relief fills your body. You retrieve the tinder box, douse your sword in oil and light it, waving it high above you. You hear a faint cheer from the forest below and know you fellow soldiers have seen you.

Your mission has been a complete success. Well done! Are you ready to face your *next adventure*?

174

You can't hear anything above the sound of your own breathing.

Head up the stairs using *Stealth*	Turn to **87**
Run up the stairs	Turn to **41**

175

The key slots into the hole and turns smoothly.

How would you like to proceed?

Enter cautiously	Turn to **126**
Enter quickly	Turn to **81**

176

You quickly retrieve and throw a dagger.

Roll 2d6 and test for *Accuracy*.

Roll 2d6 and test for *Power*.

If both tests are successful, turn to **93**. Otherwise, turn to **86**.

177

The guard sees your pendant and immediately stops.

"You wear the pendant of The Worthy. My religion forbids me to strike you."

This confuses you for a moment.

"However, the guard says, it will not stop my colleagues. Intruder!"

Caught off guard two more guards come down the stairs. You don't stand a chance and quickly succumb to their blows.

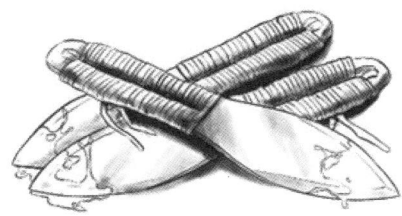

A Branching Narrative

Vents!

Simon Birks

Vents!

Welcome to the additional rules for Vents!

These rules should be used in conjunction with the 'General Rules for Adventure' and will take precedence should there be a conflict between the two.

Additional Rules

As a stowaway on board the spaceship, you begin the adventure armed with a crowbar, with a weapon damage of 2.

A Branching Narrative: Vents!

1

You wake with a start, confused by all the noise. There are at least two different alarms blaring, and you can hear people moving around on the ship.

You look towards the compartment door, worried someone may open it and see you lying amongst the light cargo. Clearly, this was not the best space faring vessel to stowaway on.

"Toxic gas detected," a computerised voice announces over the noise. "Venting required."

Then, almost immediately after it, comes another.

"Venting system malfunction."

The perfect solar storm, you think. You scan the room trying to work out your next move. You don't want to leave the compartment - a stowaway's life is risky enough without wilfully giving yourself up.

You stand and look around, and it's then you see the green gas, very slowly entering the compartment under the bottom of what should be a sealed door. Either there's something wrong with the door seal, or the gas is corrosive.

You haven't got long. If you can find a space suit, perhaps you can find safer quarters. Momentarily, you think about opening the door and trying to find the crew compartment, but you dismiss it again; you don't know the ship layout, and the corridor might be filled with gas.

That leaves the boxes in the compartment. There are five you can see. Fortunately, the crowbar you brought on board as a weapon in case you needed to threaten someone should be good enough to open most of them.

There's a large green box, a medium scarlet box, a smaller yellow box, a long purple box leaning against the wall and a sky-blue box on a shelf towards the top of the room.

The gas is at 15% Saturation already. The table below shows the effects of the gas should you remain unprotected.

Saturation	Effect
0-49%	No effect
50%	All attributes are -1
60%	All attributes are -2
70%	All attributes are -3
80%	All attributes are -4
81%+	Unconsciousness and death.

Look in the smaller yellow box	Turn to **7**
Explore the sky-blue box	Turn to **17**
Investigate the medium scarlet box	Turn to **31**
Look elsewhere	Turn to **33**
Examine the long purple box	Turn to **38**
Check the large green box	Turn to **43**

2

You prise the lid open under great strain. Inside are lines of gold bars, stacked upon each other.

You quickly remove the top two layers of bars to see if anything is under them, but there isn't.

Add 5% to the *Gas Saturation*.

What would you like to do now?

Look in the smaller yellow box	Turn to **7**
Explore the sky-blue box	Turn to **17**
Investigate the medium scarlet box	Turn to **31**
Look elsewhere	Turn to **33**
Examine the long purple box	Turn to **38**

3

The grill is secured tightly by screws. You look around the floor and see that the contents of the blue box included screwdrivers.

Roll 2d6 and test for *Detection*.

If the test is successful, turn to **12**. Otherwise, turn to **19**.

4

You dodge out of the crew member's way and step backwards. They briefly look towards the sky-blue box, before falling to the floor, breathing their last. Behind them the door closes automatically, and you hear the deadbolts engage. You won't be getting out of that door.

Turn to **27**.

5

You wait to see what will happen, and they continue to stare at the sky-blue box.

After a few more seconds, the crewmember falls to the floor, breathing their last. Behind them the door closes automatically, and you hear the deadbolts engage. You won't be getting out of that door.

Turn to **27**.

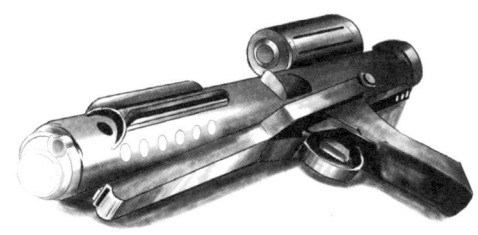

6

You search this box but find no strong tape - the gas must be playing tricks with your mind.

The gas is very strong now. You have one more chance to find the tape.

Get the tape from the sky-blue box	Turn to **18**
Get the tape from the medium scarlet box	Turn to **26**
Get the tape from the large green box	Turn to **29**
Get the tape from the small yellow box	Turn to **40**

7

The lid of this box is not even secured, and you lift the lid without the use of force. If you've not opened and taken it already, you find two rations inside (+1w). The rations will restore 3 to your Health when eaten outside of combat.

The gas continues to enter the compartment.

Add 5% to the *Gas Saturation*.

If you are still conscious, you can do one of the following:

Explore the sky-blue box	Turn to **17**
Investigate the medium scarlet box	Turn to **31**
Look elsewhere	Turn to **33**
Examine the long purple box	Turn to **38**
Check the large green box	Turn to **43**

8

You search this box but find no strong tape.

Overcome by the gas, you feel yourself consciousness, and know you won't wake up again.

9

There is nothing new to see in the purple box.

Add 5% to the *Gas Saturation*.

If you are still conscious, you can do any of the following:

Look in the smaller yellow box	Turn to **7**
Explore the sky-blue box	Turn to **17**
Investigate the medium scarlet box	Turn to **31**
Look elsewhere	Turn to **33**
Check the large green box	Turn to **43**

10

Have you found the gold bars?

If so, turn to **15**. Otherwise, turn to **25**.

11

You search this box but find no strong tape - the gas must be playing tricks with your mind.

The gas is very strong now. You have one more chance to find the tape.

Get the tape from the long purple box	Turn to **8**
Get the tape from the sky-blue box	Turn to **18**
Get the tape from the medium scarlet box	Turn to **26**
Get the tape from the large green box	Turn to **29**

12

You scramble around the floor, feeling the oxygen getting thinner and thinner.

Finally, when you think all has been lost, you find the screwdriver you were looking for.

You grab it and start to undo the screws holding the vent in place (turn to **41**).

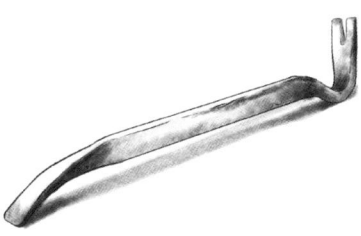

13

The box lid is firmly in place. You can attempt to open it but be aware this will take more time.

Add 5% to the *Gas Saturation*.

If you are still conscious, you can also look in the other boxes.

Look in the smaller yellow box	Turn to **7**
Explore the sky-blue box	Turn to **17**
Force the long purple box	Turn to **23**
Investigate the medium scarlet box	Turn to **31**
Look elsewhere	Turn to **33**
Check the large green box	Turn to **43**

14

The lid is locked shut, and you're not sure your crowbar is good enough to do the trick.

Add 5% to the *Gas Saturation*.

If you are still conscious, you put the crowbar between the lid and the box and use all your strength to try and pry it open.

Roll 2d6 and test for *Power*.

If the test is successful, turn to **2**. Otherwise, turn to **34**.

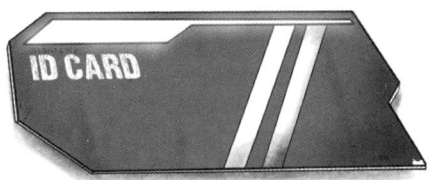

15

You push the box, which is slightly lighter now the top two layers of bars are out. Thankfully it moves, and you see a dented floor panel below it.

Add 5% to the *Gas Saturation*.

If you are still conscious, you can do one of the following:

Look in the smaller yellow box	Turn to **7**
Explore the sky-blue box	Turn to **17**
Investigate the medium scarlet box	Turn to **31**
Try and pry up the floor tile	Turn to **37**
Examine the long purple box	Turn to **38**

16

You search this box but find no strong tape - the gas must be playing tricks with your mind.

The gas is very strong now. You have one more chance to find the tape.

Get the tape from the long purple box	Turn to **8**
Get the tape from the medium scarlet box	Turn to **26**
Get the tape from the large green box	Turn to **29**
Get the tape from the small yellow box	Turn to **40**

17

You look in the sky-blue box and see it contains a range of small tools; pliers, screwdrivers, nuts and bolts. You don't notice anything that stands out.

Add 5% to the *Gas Saturation*.

If you are still conscious, you can do any of the following:

Look in the smaller yellow box	Turn to **7**
Investigate the medium scarlet box	Turn to **31**
Look elsewhere	Turn to **33**
Examine the long purple box	Turn to **38**
Check the large green box	Turn to **43**

18

You search this box but find no strong tape.

Overcome by the gas, you feel yourself consciousness, and know you won't wake up again.

19

You scramble around the floor, feeling the oxygen getting thinner and thinner.

As your frustration grows, so does your oxygen use, and before long, it's completely spent. You try and hold your breath for as long as possible, but you're just not able to find the tool you need.

Finally, you must breathe, and within moments, you have lost consciousness, never to regain it.

20

You get the mask on, and the oxygen connected very quickly.

Now, turn to **42**.

21

You step forward to help them, and they make a desperate lunge for your oxygen.

Roll 2d6 and test your *Speed*.

If the test is successful, turn to **4**. Otherwise, turn to **39**.

22

You see the gold bars inside, stacked upon each other. A fair number of them are stacked beside the box.

Add 5% to the *Gas Saturation*.

If you are still conscious, you can do one of the following:

Look in the smaller yellow box	Turn to **7**
Explore the sky-blue box	Turn to **17**
Investigate the medium scarlet box	Turn to **31**
Look elsewhere	Turn to **33**
Examine the long purple box	Turn to **38**

23

Using your crowbar, you're able to open the long purple box without too much effort. Inside is a suit, but it's a formal dinner suit, unable to help in the current situation.

Roll 2d6 and test for *Detection*.

If the test is successful, turn to **35**. Otherwise, turn to **28**.

24

You stay back. Their eyes focus on you and the oxygen mask, and they look confused and then angry. Their gaze moves towards the top of the room, where the sky-blue box sits. They hold their arms out as if they want it.

Don't help them	Turn to **5**
Give them the sky-blue box	Turn to **36**

25

This box is heavy. You attempt to move it, but nothing is going to make it budge.

Add 5% to the *Gas Saturation*.

If you're still conscious, choose an action you haven't yet done.

Look in the smaller yellow box	Turn to **7**
Explore the sky-blue box	Turn to **17**
Investigate the medium scarlet box	Turn to **31**
Look elsewhere	Turn to **33**
Examine the long purple box	Turn to **38**
Check the large green box	Turn to **43**

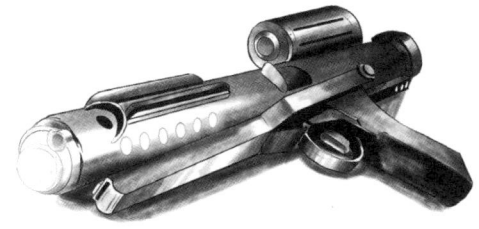

26

You open the scarlet box and grab the tape.

All this is taking time. Deduct 2 from your *Health*.

You manage to tape up the bottle in time.

You look towards the sky-blue box and wonder why the crewmember seemed interested in it.

Turn to **27**.

27

You look in the sky-blue box and see it contains a range of small tools; pliers, screwdrivers, nuts and bolts. You don't notice anything that stands out.

You are about to put it back on the shelf where you took it from when you notice there's a grill for a vent behind where the box was sitting. Perhaps this is what the crewmember was looking at. Perhaps it's a way out. At the very least, it should have oxygen in it.

You look back in the blue box and find the right screwdriver to undo the screws.

Now, turn to **41**.

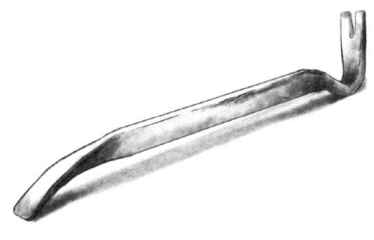

28

Frustrated you can't find anything useful, you decide to use something else.

Add 5% to *Gas Saturation*.

If you're still conscious, choose one of the following.

Look in the smaller yellow box	Turn to **7**
Explore the sky-blue box	Turn to **17**
Investigate the medium scarlet box	Turn to **31**
Look elsewhere	Turn to **33**
Check the large green box	Turn to **43**

29

You search this box but find no strong tape.

Overcome by the gas, you feel yourself consciousness, and know you won't wake up again.

30

You search this box but find no strong tape - the gas must be playing tricks with your mind.

The gas is very strong now. You have one more chance to find the tape.

Get the tape from the long purple box	Turn to **8**
Get the tape from the sky-blue box	Turn to **18**
Get the tape from the medium scarlet box	Turn to **26**
Get the tape from the small yellow box	Turn to **40**

31

You open the scarlet box and realise it's nothing more than a toolbox containing larger tools, some strong tape which is almost used up and some cable ties. Nothing looks overly important.

Add 5% to *Gas Saturation*.

If you're still conscious, choose from the following:

Look in the smaller yellow box	Turn to **7**
Explore the sky-blue box	Turn to **17**
Look elsewhere	Turn to **33**
Examine the long purple box	Turn to **38**
Check the large green box	Turn to **43**

32

You get the mask on, and the oxygen connected, but not as quickly as you'd like.

Add 5% to the *Gas Saturation*.

If you are still conscious, turn to **42**.

33

It's unlikely anyone's packed an extra space suit in the hold, so you decide to check the floor and walls. To your right, screen flashes red with unhelpful diagnostic information. The wall, apart from the door, is solid, smooth metal. You look down; square metal tiles about two feet wide cover the floor. They all look the same, apart from one which is partially under the large green box, which is set slightly askew.

Add 5% to the *Gas Saturation*.

If you are still conscious, you can do one of the following:

Look in the smaller yellow box	Turn to **7**
Try and move the big green box	Turn to **10**
Explore the sky-blue box	Turn to **17**
Investigate the medium scarlet box	Turn to **31**
Examine the long purple box	Turn to **38**
Check the large green box	Turn to **43**

34

You're unable to open the box this time.

Add 5% to the *Gas Saturation*.

If you are still conscious, you can choose one of the following:

Look in the smaller yellow box	Turn to **7**
Explore the sky-blue box	Turn to **17**
Investigate the medium scarlet box	Turn to **31**
Look elsewhere	Turn to **33**
Examine the long purple box	Turn to **38**
Check the large green box	Turn to **43**

35

The suit might be useful after all. You grab it off its hangar and stuff is at the foot of the door. It's not perfect, but you can ignore the next 2 gas saturation increases.

You can do any of the following.

Look in the smaller yellow box	Turn to **7**
Explore the sky-blue box	Turn to **17**
Investigate the medium scarlet box	Turn to **31**
Look elsewhere	Turn to **33**
Check the large green box	Turn to **43**

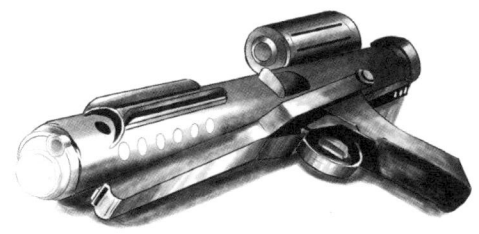

36

You reach up and take the sky-blue box from the shelf and hold it out to them. They look confused and feebly knock it out of your hands. The box falls to the floor and its contents clatter to the ground. Their eyes return to the shelf and when you look you can make out a grill cover the air conditioning vent.

The crewmember falls to the floor, breathing their last. At least you have a way out. Behind them the door closes automatically, and you hear the deadbolts engage. You won't be getting out of that door.

Turn to **3**.

37

You put the crowbar under the tile and lever it up without any effort. Underneath you find a plain box which you pull out open.

The box houses an old oxygen mask, a bit worse for wear, but usable, and a small oxygen bottle under the clothes.

Add 5% to the *Gas Saturation*.

If you are still conscious, you must roll 2d6 and test your *Speed*.

If the test is successful, turn to **20**. Otherwise, turn to **32**.

38

Have you already opened the long purple box?

If so, turn to **9**. Otherwise, turn to **13**.

39

You try to move but you're not quick enough. They knock the bottle off from your back and it severs the already perishing tube.

The crew member looks towards the top of the room, where the sky-blue box sits and try to raise their arms as if they want it. You see their eyes roll up into their sockets and they fall to the floor, dead. Behind them the door closes automatically, and you hear the deadbolts engage. You won't be getting out of that door.

The gas is strong now, and you're finding it very difficult to breathe. You must try and fix your oxygen supply.

Have you seen some strong tape you might use in one of the boxes?

Get the tape from the long purple box	Turn to **6**
Get the tape from the small yellow box	Turn to **11**
Get the tape from the sky-blue box	Turn to **16**
Get the tape from the medium scarlet box	Turn to **26**
Get the tape from the large green box	Turn to **30**

40

You search this box but find no strong tape.

Overcome by the gas, you feel yourself consciousness, and know you won't wake up again.

41

Within a few moments, the vent is off, and you are climbing into the space beyond. Once again, the computerised voice announces the following in quick succession.

"Toxic gas detected. Venting required."

"Venting system malfunction."

Perhaps there's a way to fix the venting system. You have experience of ships onboard systems; if you hadn't, you'd have been caught long ago.

One of the rooms off the vents will house a terminal you can use.

You aren't sure of the ship's layout, so when the vent splits you go right on a gut feeling. A few feet in, you find a grill, through which you can see the galley. Not the most useful room, but at least it has a terminal.

You can't see any crew, so punch down on the grate and watch it fall to the floor below. You drop down quickly and take in the situation.

There is less gas in here, but you keep your mask on and your oxygen connected. In the back of your mind, you note you should try and get a replacement bottle soon.

The galley is large and includes a seated area for food consumption. To the left is the galley counter with a sink, cooker, and cupboards. There seems to be something disassembled at the far end. Four desks sit against the wall to the right, with a terminal on each. In the centre there are two tables. One has an open manual on it, whilst the other has a plate of half-eaten food.

Check out the half-eaten food	Turn to **79**
Investigate the desk area	Turn to **87**
Investigate the open manual	Turn to **137**
Investigate the counter area	Turn to **182**

42

The oxygen should keep you alive for a while. Under different circumstances you might wonder why someone has stashed a space suit under the floor, but for now you're just thankful.

You quickly recover from the effects of the gas; restore all your attributes to their starting values.

Perhaps now would be a good time to explore the ship...

Without warning the door opens behind you and step backwards.

Standing in the doorway is a crew member clutching their throat.

Go and help them	Turn to **21**
Leave them alone	Turn to **24**

43

Have you already opened the Green Box?

If so, turn to **22**. Otherwise, turn to **14**.

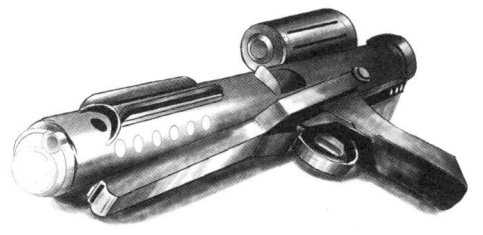

44

You push the grate but its stuck fast.

Roll 2d6 and test for *Power*.

If the test is successful, turn to **58**. Otherwise, turn to **65**.

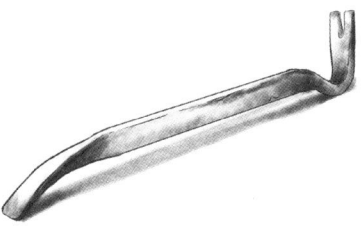

45

You roll out the way as a bolt from the blaster whizzes over your head.

Now, turn to **83**.

46

Off to the right you notice the suit the crew member had been wearing, discarded and empty.

It appears one of the bodies might not be as dead as it looks.

Not wanting to use a weapon that fires or explodes, you retrieve your crowbar.

Attack the body on the left	Turn to **71**
Attack the body in the centre	Turn to **92**
Attack the body on the right	Turn to **133**

47

You stand your ground and listen as the crew member gets closer.

The door opens and they step into the room.

Turn to **142**.

48

You open the cupboard door above the sink. Inside you find plates and cups. One of the cups is turned over, as if it's captured something underneath.

Pick the cup up	Turn to **57**
Check out the half-eaten food	Turn to **79**
Investigate the desk area	Turn to **87**
Open the cupboard below the sink	Turn to **103**
Investigate the open manual	Turn to **137**
Check out the disassembled gizmo at the end	Turn to **185**

49

You move as far away from the door as you can and wait to see if the gas stops.

Unfortunately, it doesn't.

Use a proximity mine if you have one	Turn to **68**
Use the blaster if you have one	Turn to **160**
Use the pesticide if you have it	Turn to **172**
Otherwise	Turn to **81**

50

The gas has reached you, and you must head toward the left of the corridor as quickly as possible.

Roll 2d6 and test for *Speed*.

If the test is successful, turn to **63**. Otherwise, turn to **184**.

51

You duck into the crew area and close the door behind you. You're pleased to see the seal around the door keeps the gas out.

The crew area consists of a bunk and a small bedside table with two drawers. There is a door opposite you, and a bundle of clothes to the left of the door.

Search the clothes	Turn to **59**
Open the door	Turn to **89**
Check the drawers	Turn to **183**
Investigate the bunk	Turn to **196**

52

You back away from the door and wait. The holes stop appearing, but the gas continues to be pumped.

You can see some movement through the holes in the door, and finally the crew member moves off.

You wait a moment to be sure they're gone and then open the door. To the left, towards the rear of the ship, you see them trying to fix something. The door to the bridge opens beside you, and they look around. Quickly you jump through it, before they have time to react.

Turn to **179**.

53

Something jogs your memory that you've seen a system like this before, and you remember if you hit the back key, it won't log you out.

Turn to **144**.

54

You see the word Huckle85 before the words disappear and replaced with the message 'Terminal locked for 30:00' and begins to countdown.

By the thinness of the oxygen you're breathing, you need to do something quickly.

Plug in the unplugged terminal	Turn to **192**
Examine the terminal on the right	Turn to **122**

55

As you're about to turn away, you notice a corner of something sticking out on the bottom shelf.

When you pick it up you see it's an ID card (**+1w**) that someone has dropped. It might come in handy.

You can now investigate the fridge or go to the door.

Check the fridge	Turn to **132**
Go to the door	Turn to **114**

56

You wait and listen as they approach the door. It opens and they step inside, but your cover wasn't good enough, and before you have time to use the spray, they push you away.

Now, turn to **142**.

57

Carefully, you pick the cup up. Underneath, you find a small piece of paper with the word 'J-gh1xj0q-9'.

It looks like a password.

Check out the half-eaten food	Turn to 79
Investigate the desk area	Turn to 87
Open the cupboard below the sink	Turn to 103
Investigate the open manual	Turn to 137
Check out the disassembled gizmo at the end	Turn to 185

58

The grate swings open just in the time, as you see gas is nearly upon you.

You close the door behind you, stopping the gas in its tracks.

You turn and see you are in the medical bay of the ship, which fortunately has no gas in it. It's not exactly up to cleanliness standards, but you see a full oxygen cylinder (**+4w**) and mask that you can take, should you need it later.

There are cupboards on the wall and what appears to be a large fridge opposite you.

The door to the rest of the ship is to your right.

Go to the door	Turn to **114**
Check the fridge	Turn to **132**
Investigate the cupboards	Turn to **141**

59

You sift through the clothes and find nothing of use.

Roll 2d6 and test for *Detection*.

If the test is successful, turn to **138**. Otherwise, turn to **69**.

60

Hoping to catch them off guard, you grab the space suit and pull them towards you, whilst attempting to spin and change places with them.

Unfortunately, you're not quick enough, and you hear the blaster, and feel the heat of the bolt just before you succumb to your mortality.

61

After about fifteen feet, you reach the end of the vent. Through the slats you can see little of the room beyond.

Try and force the grate	Turn to **147**
Turn back and investigate the control panel	Turn to **162**
Turn back and head left along the tunnel	Turn to **136**

62

You don't catch the words before they disappear and replaced with the message 'Terminal locked for 30:00' and begins to countdown.

By the thinness of the oxygen you're breathing, you need to do something quickly.

Examine the terminal on the right	Turn to **122**
Plug the unplugged terminal in	Turn to **192**

63

You crawl away from the gas, though can't help but inhale a little.

Deduct 2 from your *Health*.

Turn to **136**.

64

You insert the silver key and turn it successfully.

The top drawer has some personal effects, including a pass card (+1w).

Now, turn to **128**.

65

You try to open the door, but it doesn't budge. The gas is surrounding you now, and you hold your breath, frantically trying to kick the door open.

Still, it doesn't budge. No longer able to hold your breath you can do nothing about your demise.

66

You take a moment to look at the broken terminals.

One of them is completely bust, and has been harvested for parts, but the other one is just not plugged in.

Examine the terminal on the right	Turn to **122**
Plug the terminal in	Turn to **192**
Examine the terminal on the left	Turn to **150**

67

The bugs swarm towards you.

Roll 2d6 and test your *Speed*.

Roll 2d6 and test your *Accuracy*.

If both tests are successful, turn to **176**. Otherwise, turn to **88**.

68

You take one of the proximity mines and put it on the door. You hit the armed switch, which counts down from five.

Roll 2d6 and test your *Speed*.

If the test is successful, turn to **159**. Otherwise, turn to **96**.

69

You notice nothing of any great importance and throw the clothes back into the corner.

Open the door	Turn to **89**
Investigate the bunk	Turn to **196**
Check the drawers	Turn to **183**

70

You turn to head back out into the ship, but something catches your eye as you turn. You immediately stop and watch as the seat on the right turns and the crew member stands up to fight.

Turn to **164**.

71

You swing the crowbar at the seated body on the left. It hits it without flinching. They were already dead.

You hear a noise behind you.

Roll 2d6 and test for *Speed*.

If the test is successful, turn to **115**. Otherwise, turn to **130**.

72

You're not sure what you should do next.

Examine the terminal on the left	Turn to **191**
Check the broken terminals	Turn to **108**
Press the back key	Turn to **144**

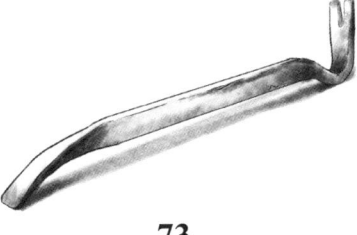

73

You run your hands quickly along the walls and floor in the near-darkness and think you feel something out of place.

Annoyed you were going so fast you try and find it again.

Roll 2d6 and test for *Detection*.

If the test is successful, turn to **199**. Otherwise, turn to **101**.

74

You spray the pesticide in the direction of the crew member.

Roll 2d6 and test for *Accuracy*.

If the test is successful, turn to **169**. Otherwise, turn to **120**.

75

You search the corridor for the crew member, but can't find a trace of them, though the blood you can see means at least you wounded them.

The back part of the ship is blocked with twisted metal, so the only option is to enter the bridge.

Turn to **178**.

76

The gas has made your head woozy, and you hit the 'No' key by mistake.

You try and keep breathing the oxygen canister is empty. You fall to your knees gasping, feeling the poison burn your lungs. Fortunately, you lose consciousness with the second breath, and don't wake up.

77

The words 'Terminal locked for 28:56' are displayed and the numbers are counting down.

Your oxygen is nearly empty.

Examine the broken terminals	Turn to **190**
Investigate the terminal on the right	Turn to **165**

78

You jump into the dark room and hit the button by the door to secure it. You hear it thud and deadlock and breathe a sigh of relief.

Alone in the near darkness, it takes a moment for your eyes to adjust, and you hear your foe walking up the corridor towards you.

You can make out two cupboards, one long and one stubby, attached to the wall nearby, a swipe card reader next to both.

Investigate the stubby locker	Turn to **186**
Investigate the long locker	Turn to **167**
Search the room more	Turn to **173**

79

You investigate the plate of food. It seems to mostly be warmed up pureed food. Nothing very nutritious there.

Roll 2d6 and test for *Detection*.

If the test is successful, turn to **151**. Otherwise, turn to **188**.

80

You wait and listen as they approach the door. It opens and they step inside. Swiftly you pull the visor up on their suit and spray the pesticide directly into their face. Turn to **169**.

81

Try as you might to hold onto your breath, the gas quickly overwhelms you. You fall to the floor unconscious, never to be regained.

82

Hoping to catch them off guard, you grab the space suit and pull them towards you, whilst attempting to spin and change places with them.

Amazingly it works and you're able to push them into the engine room and run further down the corridor.

Turn to **156**.

83

They didn't even stop and ask who you were.

The blaster is not a weapon you can face up against; it's only a matter of time before they hit you.

Fortunately, you rolled next to a vertical vent in the wall that has opened and is blowing oxygen into the room. You don't have time to think about your next move and jump into the vent and drop to the floor below.

The suit the crew member is wearing is too big to fit in the vent and it'd take a while for them to take it off.

You fall about six feet before landing on the metal grating beneath. The horizontal tunnel runs left to right. Nearby, on the side of the tunnel, is a small control panel with several buttons on.

You must act quickly to get out of the line of fire from above.

Head left along the tunnel	Turn to **177**
Head right along the tunnel	Turn to **61**
Investigate the control panel	Turn to **162**

84

You look out of the window in the door and see the corridor is clear and the door to one of the crew quarters closing.

Though you're not sure what to do next, being in the engine room isn't going to help you.

Without a second thought you quickly move down the corridor, as quietly as possible.

Turn to **156**.

85

You enter Huckle85 into the login name and press enter.

A new prompt appears beneath:
'Password:'

If you found a password, go to the section number found in the password by reading the numbers left to right.

86

You look over the ship controls, trying to find something that might help you. Nothing is obvious and before you can do anything else you hear the door open behind you.

Now, turn to **142**.

87

There are four desks, each with a terminal on it. Two of the terminals appear to be off, with a sign on them saying 'Broken'.

Of the two that are on, you can hear a noise coming from the left terminal, but the right one seems quiet.

Examine the terminal on the left	Turn to **170**
Examine the terminal on the right	Turn to **122**
Examine the broken terminals	Turn to **66**

88

You move backwards but trip and fall. The bugs are on you in seconds, biting at your mask and your oxygen pipe. Even though they appear to be weakening, it's too late. After a couple of inhalations, you lose consciousness, never to regain it.

89

The door is unlocked and slides open to reveal a corridor filled with doors. It looks like there might be more crew quarters in front of you and immediately to your right, judging by the names on the door.

The back of the ship is to the right, and the front is to the left. The doors off the corridor just to the left of you lead to the two docking bays.

Head towards the back of the ship	Turn to **131**
Head towards the front	Turn to **156**

90

You put the two wires together and an electric shock knocks you backwards.

Deduct 2 from your *Health*.

Reduce your *Accuracy* by 1.

Now, turn to **50**.

91

You put the mask on and watch as more holes appear in the door and more gas is pumped in.

You could try and retaliate now or wait and see.

Use a blaster if you have one	Turn to **160**
Use the pesticide if you have it	Turn to **172**
Use a proximity mine if you have one	Turn to **68**
Wait and see	Turn to **52**

92

You swing the crowbar at the seated body on the left. It hits it without flinching. They were already dead.

You hear a noise behind you.

Roll 2d6 and test for *Speed*.

If the test is successful, turn to **115**. Otherwise, turn to **130**.

93

There's nothing like a challenge!

Roll 2d6 and test for *Detection*.

If the test is successful, turn to **198**. Otherwise, turn to **149**.

94

You duck down behind the door, and hope whoever's in the lift doesn't come looking for you.

You hear the elevator door open, and footsteps leading up to the engine room. The door opens and you see the crew member standing there.

Roll 2d6 and test for *Speed*.

If the test is successful, turn to **82**. Otherwise, turn to **60**.

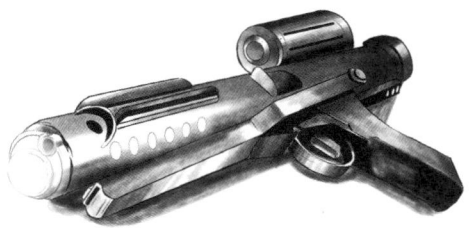

95

You raise your crowbar and bring it down on the call button, with no effect. Then you try and open the doors in front of you, but they're stuck fast.

The elevator is nearly here, leaving you with only one choice.

Turn to **121**.

96

You turn and run as quickly as possible but are unable to avoid the blast altogether.

Deduct 4 from your *Health*.

Are you wearing an oxygen mask?

If so, turn to **75**. Otherwise, turn to **110**.

97

Ever you're amazed by the accuracy of your shot under such circumstances.

The bolt hits them square in the chest and slices right through them. They go down, dead.

The bolt keeps on travelling though and impacts the side of the ship. There's damage, but it's not catastrophic.

Now, turn to **200**.

98

You try and open the locker but it's too strong for you.

Investigate the stubby locker	Turn to **194**
Search the room more	Turn to **173**

99

You put the two wires together and an electric shock knocks you backwards.

Deduct 2 from your *Health*.

Reduce your *Accuracy* by 1.

Now, turn to **50**.

100

The bolt hits the door, but part of it rebounds back into the room.

Roll 2d6 and test for *Speed*.

If the test is successful, turn to **119**. Otherwise, turn to **168**.

101

Unable to find it again you curse your impatience.

Suddenly, you hear the enemy outside the door. The space outside is too small for them to use the blaster safely, but you hear another, high pitch, noise which sounds like a laser cutter.

Within seconds you see a hole open in the door, and then gas starts to enter the room.

Have you found a fresh gas mask and cylinder?

If so, turn to **91**. Otherwise, turn to **140**.

102

Quickly, you spray the pesticide in their direction, and its effects are instant. The bugs stop in their tracks and appear to dissolve. Whatever the Pesticide is, you don't want it touching you.

You have enough Pesticide left for one more spray.

Not wanting to approach the counter again, you have the following choices.

Investigate the desk area	Turn to **87**
Investigate the open manual	Turn to **137**
Check out the half-eaten food	Turn to **79**

103

You open the cupboard door below the sink, expecting to find food. As soon as the seal is broken however, a swarm of Billut Bugs fly out. These are ravenous beasts with a sharp set of teeth. You must keep away from them.

Do you have a Sprayer?

If so, turn to **146**. Otherwise, turn to **67**.

104

You attempt to hide behind the door in the darkness.

Roll 2d6 and test for *Stealth*.

If the test is successful, turn to **80**. Otherwise, turn to **56**.

105

You notice an indentation on the page of the manual. Holding it up to the light, it appears someone has rested against the book to write something down.

After careful examination, you see the characters - 'J-gh1xj0q-9'.

It might be a password.

As you think about your next move, one of the terminals on the desks makes a noise.

Turn to **87**.

106

You approach the space between the engines and realise one of them is running hot. You're going to have to be careful not to hurt yourself. Still, there's little you can do now.

Roll 2d6 and test for *Accuracy*.

If the test is successful, turn to **180**. Otherwise, turn to **155**.

107

You put the two wires together and hear the lock mechanism whirr. The door opens and beyond you can see what looks like a crew member sleeping area.

The gas has almost reached you.

Enter the crew area	Turn to **51**
Head left along the vent	Turn to **136**

108

One of them is completely bust, and has been harvested for parts, but the other one is just not plugged in.

You try and keep breathing the oxygen canister is empty. You fall to your knees gasping, feeling the poison burn your lungs. Fortunately, you lose consciousness with the second breath, and don't wake up.

109

The screen goes blank for a moment, and then a message appears:

'Gas detected in galley - extract?'

Turn to **135**.

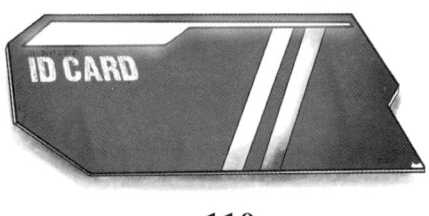

110

The gas begins to dissipate from the blast, but not quickly enough.

Deduct 4 from your *Health*.

You search the corridor for the crew member, but can't find a trace of them, though the blood you can see means that at least you wounded them.

The back part of the ship is blocked with twisted metal, so the only option is to enter the bridge.

Turn to **178**.

111

It was always going to be a difficult throw.

The mine misses the crew member and attaches to the hull of the ship. Within a few seconds it detonates, causing an explosion that takes half of the front of it away.

You can't do anything as you are sucked into the blackness of space.

112

You place the proximity mine on the door, arm it and stand well back.

You hear the footsteps approach the door and watch as it opens. The suited crew member looks towards you for a moment before the mine goes off, punching a hole in their chest. They fall, dead.

There is some damage to the ship, but nothing catastrophic.

Now, turn to **200**.

113

Seeing the situation getting desperate, if you have one of the following, you can use it.

Set a proximity mine	Turn to **143**
Use the blaster	Turn to **181**
Use the pesticide	Turn to **74**
Otherwise	Turn to **174**

114

The door is unlocked and slides open to reveal a corridor filled with doors. To the right are doors to docking bays, and beyond that, doors to crew quarters, judging by the name plates you can make out on the door.

The back of the ship is to the far right. You assume the door to the bridge is on your left. There is another door in front of you.

Head towards the back of the ship	Turn to **131**
Investigate the front of the ship	Turn to **152**

115

You move out the way quickly, and feel the air move past your head as something brushes by it.

You turn and face your attacker.

Turn to **164**.

116

You manoeuvre into the small space between the engines, but you can feel your leg hurting almost immediately.

Deduct 2 from your *Health*.

Deduct 1 from your *Stealth*.

You hear the elevator door open, and footsteps leading up to the engine room. The door opens and you hold your breath. Fortunately, the door closes, and you hear footsteps walking away.

You emerge from the space and think about your next move. Turn to **84**.

117

You put the two wires together and an electric shock knocks you backwards.

Deduct 2 from your *Health*.

Reduce your *Accuracy* by 1.

Now, turn to **50**.

118

You begin making your way back down the corridor but have no sooner started then you see traces of the gas coming into the vent at the end.

You can still reach the control panel you saw earlier.

> Investigate the control panel   Turn to **162**
> Head back left along the tunnel   Turn to **136**

119

The bolt glances off your leg.

Deduct 2 from your *Health*.

Are you wearing an oxygen mask?

If so, turn to **75**. Otherwise, turn to **110**.

120

Some of the pesticide hits the crew member in the face and they stagger backwards a little, clearly disorientated.

You must now continue to fight them.

	Speed	*Accuracy*	*Damage*	*Health*
Crew Member	8	8	2	7

If you win, turn to **200**.

121

The door to the Engine room is unlocked and you step into the room, pleased to see there is no gas here.

The door closes behind you. In the corridor, you hear the elevator arrive - it might be the crew member who attacked you earlier.

This room is small, with few places to hide. There are three engines, with a small gap between each. Alternatively, you can hide behind the door.

Duck down behind the door	Turn to **94**
Hide between engines 1 & 2	Turn to **106**
Hide between engines 2 & 3	Turn to **145**

122

The terminal on the right appears to be already logged in. There is a diagram of the ship's lower floor. The Weapons Store is highlighted with a message 'Lights Malfunction'.

Investigate plans more	Turn to **165**
Examine the terminal on the left	Turn to **77**
Press the back key	Turn to **144**
Examine the broken terminals	Turn to **148**

123

It was always going to be a difficult shot.

The bolt hits the crew member, and kills them immediately, but it also travels through the hull of the ship, causing an explosion that takes half of the front of it away.

You can't do anything as you are sucked into the blackness of space.

124

On closer inspection it appears to be a liquid sprayer. It's in quite a few parts and doesn't look easy to assemble.

Try and assemble the sprayer	Turn to **93**
Open the cupboard above the sink	Turn to **48**
Open the cupboard below the sink	Turn to **103**
Investigate the desk area	Turn to **87**
Check out the open manual	Turn to **137**
Check out the half-eaten food	Turn to **79**

125

You put the two wires together and an electric shock knocks you backwards.

Deduct 2 from your *Health*.

Reduce your *Accuracy* by 1.

Now, turn to **50**.

126

You swipe the card in the reader and hear a clunk as the door unlocks. Pulling the door open you can make out a blaster (+4w). The read out tells you it has four shots. Experience tells you it will do a lot of damage.

Investigate the stubby locker	Turn to **194**
Search the room more	Turn to **173**

127

It's difficult but you fit in the gap between the engines.

You hear footsteps leading up to the engine room. The door opens and you hold your breath. After a few seconds, the door closes, and you hear footsteps walking away.

You emerge from the space and think about your next move.

Now, turn to **84**.

128

Before you have the chance to search more, you notice some gas is entering via the grate after all. Now would be the time to leave.

Turn to **89**.

129

You try and open the locker but it's too strong for you.

Investigate the long locker	Turn to **194**
Search the room more	Turn to **173**

130

You try and move out of the way but get caught on the shoulder by a heavy implement.

Deduct 3 from your *Health*.

You turn and face your attacker. Turn to **164**.

131

You begin to make your way towards the back of the ship, past the crew doors.

The last door in front of you is to the engines, the one to the left is for the elevator to the floor above, and the one to the right is to Engineering.

Check the lift	Turn to **195**
Check the engineering door	Turn to **187**
Check the engines door	Turn to **121**

132

You open the large fridge door and see shelf upon shelf of test tubes and petri dishes.

On one of the bottom shelves, someone has stowed a couple of syringes (+2w each). The label on the syringes says Griggan. You know what this is, though it is illegal.

Griggan will temporarily increase all your abilities by +2 for the next ability test only.

Go to the door	Turn to **114**
Investigate the cupboards	Turn to **166**

133

You swing the crowbar at the seated body on the right. They move before it connects and stand to attack you.

Turn to **164**.

134

You put the two wires together and an electric current shocks you backwards.

Deduct 2 from your *Health*.

Reduce your *Accuracy* by 1.

Now, turn to **50**.

135

You hit the 'Yes' key and hear the hiss of the extractor fans as the suck the gas out of the room, replacing it a moment later with air. You rip the oxygen mask off and breathe in deeply.

No sooner have you had a moment to thank the gods, when a door opens and you see a crew member in a space suit entering equipped with a blaster, aimed at you.

Roll 2d6 and test for *Speed*.

If the test is successful, turn to **45**. Otherwise, turn to **139**.

136

With little other option you try and force the grate at the end.

Turn to **44**.

137

You go over to the table and look at the manual. The page it is open at displays a lock mechanism and has instructions for overriding the mechanism by detaching the front and joining the internal purple and the black wires together.

Roll 2d6 and test for *Detection*.

If the test is successful, turn to **105**. Otherwise, turn to **189**.

138

You notice one of the side panels has some scratching next to it, and it comes away easily when you pull it.

Behind the panel, someone has stashed oxygen mask and full oxygen canister (**+4w**).

Check the drawers	Turn to **183**
Investigate the bunk	Turn to **196**
Open the door	Turn to **89**

139

You roll out of the way, but the bolt clips your arm.

Deduct 2 from your *Health*.

Now, turn to **83**.

140

You think about blocking the hole, but another one appears and then another, with more gas being injected into the room.

Running out of options, and with no obvious vent to escape in, you consider your choices.

Use the blaster if you have one	Turn to **160**
Use a proximity mine if you have one	Turn to **68**
Use the pesticide if you have it	Turn to **172**
Move far away from the door	Turn to **49**

141

The cupboards are all unlocked, thankfully. Most of what you find are medicines and medical utensils.

Roll 2d6 and test for *Detection*.

If the test is successful, turn to **55**. Otherwise, turn to **153**.

142

You have no choice but to fight the suited crew member.

	Speed	Accuracy	Damage	Health
Suited Crew	9	9	3	19

If your health reduces to 3 during the battle, turn to **113**. If you win without your Health being reduced to 3 or under, turn to **200**.

143

Desperately, you arm and throw the proximity mine in the direction of the crew member.

Roll 2d6 and test for *Accuracy*.

If the test is successful, turn to **163**. Otherwise, turn to **111**.

144

Finding it difficult to concentrate you hit the back key, which takes you to a screen which says, 'Gas detected in galley - extract?'

Roll 2d6 and test for *Accuracy*.

If the test is successful, turn to **135**. Otherwise, turn to **76**.

145

You approach the gap between engine 2 & 3. There's hardly any space there at all; it's going to be a struggle.

Roll 2d6 and test your *Stealth*.

If the test is successful, turn to **127**. Otherwise, turn to **116**.

146

Has it got Pesticide in it?

If so, turn to **102**. Otherwise, turn to **67**.

147

You push open the grate and are shocked to see three bodies on the floor by the door. Gas fills the room, and you must turn and head away quickly.

Roll 2d6 and test for *Speed*.

If the test is successful, turn to **63**. Otherwise, turn to **184**.

148

You take a moment to look at the broken terminals. One of them is completely bust, and has been harvested for parts, but the other one is just not plugged in.

You can feel the air is getting thin in your oxygen tank.

Examine the terminal on the left	Turn to **77**
Plug the terminal in	Turn to **192**

149

You try your very best, but it simply won't go together.

Investigate the open manual	Turn to **137**
Investigate the desk area	Turn to **87**
Open the cupboard above the sink	Turn to **48**
Open the cupboard below the sink	Turn to **103**
Check out the half-eaten food	Turn to **79**

150

Something is on the screen and then flashes off.

Roll 2d6 and test for *Speed*.

If the test is successful, turn to **54**. Otherwise, turn to **62**.

151

You notice something glimmering in the food. Using the fork, you separate the food and find a silver key (**+1w**).

You can't see anything else of importance.

As you think about your next move, one of the terminals on the desks makes a noise.

Turn to **87**.

152

As soon as you step into the corridor, a door opens towards the rear of the ship and the crew member emerges, blaster in hand.

Fortunately, two doors open next to you. One is the bridge, but the other one is dark, and you can't see what it houses.

Head into the bridge	Turn to **179**
Jump into the dark room	Turn to **78**

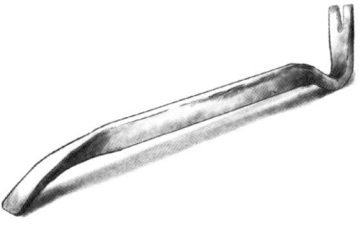

153

You close the cupboards, annoyed you haven't found anything.

You can now investigate the fridge or go to the door.

Check the fridge	Turn to **132**
Go to the door	Turn to **114**

154

You swipe the card in the reader and hear a clunk as the door unlocks. Pulling the door open you can make out a proximity mine (**+3w**) inside. This could be useful if you're accurate with it.

Investigate the long locker	Turn to **194**
Search the room more	Turn to **173**

155

You manoeuvre into the small space between the engines but catch your arm on the engine.

Deduct 2 from your *Health*.

Deduct 1 from your *Accuracy*.

You hear footsteps leading up to the engine room. The door opens and you hold your breath. After a few moments, the door closes, and you hear footsteps walking away.

You emerge from the space and think about your next move.

Turn to **84**.

156

No sooner have you made it to the front of the ship, than the crew member emerges into the corridor, blaster in hand.

Fortunately, two doors open next to you. One is the bridge, but the other one is dark, and you can't see what it houses.

Head into the bridge	Turn to **179**
Jump into the dark room	Turn to **78**

157

You position yourself behind the empty chair and line up the blaster with the door.

You hear footsteps approach the door and watch as it opens. The suited crew member looks at you for a moment before you press the trigger and the bolt shoots out, punching a hole in their chest. They fall, dead.

There is some damage to the ship, but nothing catastrophic.

Now, turn to **200**.

158

You cannot find anything else in the room.

Suddenly, you hear the enemy outside the door. The space outside is too small for them to use the blaster safely, but you hear another, high pitch, noise which sounds like a laser cutter.

Within seconds you see a hole open in the door, and then gas starts to enter the room.

Have you found a fresh gas mask and cylinder?

If so, turn to **91**. Otherwise, turn to **140**.

159

You manage to get far enough away when the proximity mine detonates. The door is blasted outwards.

Are you wearing an oxygen mask?

If so, turn to **75**. Otherwise, turn to **110**.

160

It's going to be risky to fire the blaster in such a small space.

You line up the shot to hit the softest part of the door and fire.

Roll 2d6 and test for *Accuracy*.

If the test is successful, turn to **197**. Otherwise, turn to **100**.

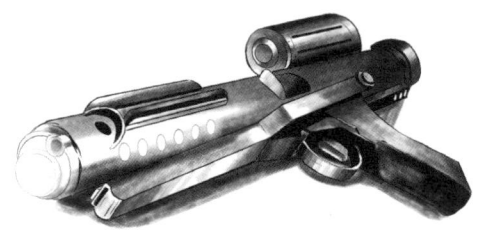

161

You don't notice anything strange about the room.

Investigate the bodies	Turn to **171**
Check the panels for information	Turn to **193**
Continue searching the ship	Turn to **70**

162

The control panel controls a lock mechanism which is attached to a door in the vent. You take off the front and can see a set of wires with numbers next to them.

Green 41
Purple 49
Black 58
Blue 76

As you look at the wires you see movement to your right. When you look you notice gas is coming into the vent.

You may have come across instructions on opening a door mechanism. If so, you are welcome to try and jury-rig the door by putting two of the different coloured wires together. If you choose to do so, add the number next to the two colours and turn to that section.

Green and Purple	Turn to **90**
Green and Black	Turn to **99**
Green and Blue	Turn to **117**
Purple and Black	Turn to **107**
Purple and Blue	Turn to **125**
Black and Blue	Turn to **134**
Head left along the tunnel	Turn to **136**

163

Ever you're amazed by the accuracy of your throw under such circumstances. The mine attaches to the ceiling right above them, and detonates a couple of seconds after, killing the crew member.

There's damage, but as there is a floor above, it's not catastrophic.

Now, turn to **200**.

164

You must fight the wounded crew member.

	Speed	Accuracy	Damage	Health
Crew Member	10	10	3	16

If your health reduces to 3 during the battle, turn to **113**. If you win without your Health being reduced to 3 or under, turn to **200**

165

You press the menu key on the right-hand terminal, and the only option you have is to log out.

Your oxygen is almost completely gone.

Roll 2d6 and test for *Detection*.

If the test is successful, turn to **53**. Otherwise, turn to **72**.

166

The cupboards are all unlocked, thankfully. Most of what you find are medicines and medical utensils.

Concerned with the amount of time you're taking, you leave the room.

Turn to **114**.

167

Do you have a keycard?

If so, turn to **126**. Otherwise, turn to **98**.

168

The bolt hits you squarely in the leg.

Deduct 5 from your *Health*.

Are you wearing an oxygen mask?

If so, turn to **75**. Otherwise, turn to **110**.

169

The whole of the pesticide hits the crew members face and they immediately stagger backwards holding their throat.

You grip the crowbar harder in your hand ready to deliver a decisive blow, but they fall heavily to the floor dead.

Now, turn to **200**.

170

You examine the terminal on the left. The screen reads 'Login attempt timeout in 10 seconds' and is counting down.

Below the message you read the following:

Login: Huckle85
Password: *******

You press the backspace key, but the keyboard is not responsive.

By the thinness of the oxygen you're breathing, you need to do something quickly.

Examine the broken terminals   Turn to **66**
Examine the terminal on the right   Turn to **122**

171

You walk over to the body in the centre to see if you can glean any information from them. As you check their pockets, you hear a noise behind you.

Roll 2d6 and test for *Speed*.

If the test is successful, turn to **115**. Otherwise, turn to **130**.

172

You retrieve the pesticide and start to pump it back through one of the holes.

Nothing happens.

If you have an oxygen mask on, turn to **52**. Otherwise, turn to **81**.

173

The room is dark.

Roll 2d6 and test for *Detection*.

If the test is successful, turn to **73**. Otherwise, turn to **158**.

174

The crew member, emboldened by your state, steps forward, and deals the mortal blow.

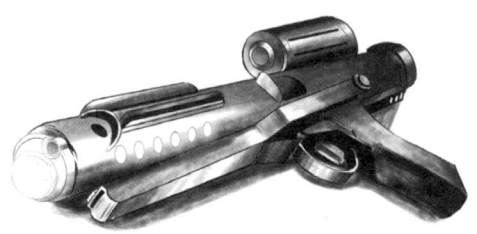

175

You run the water tap and fill the canister up. When you reattach it to the sprayer, a panel lights up 'H20 Detected - Adding Pesticide'. The water turns a green colour.

The Sprayer now weighs (**+4w**) - adjust your equipment sheet.

Investigate the desk area	Turn to **87**
Investigate the open manual	Turn to **137**
Open the cupboard above the sink	Turn to **48**
Open the cupboard below the sink	Turn to **103**
Check out the half-eaten food	Turn to **79**

176

You quickly move backwards, swerving between the tables. You're running out of space, and just when you think they're going to reach you, they slow and finally stop. It seems the gas is toxic to them, too. Within moments they are all dead on the floor.

Not wanting to go near the counters again, you have the following choices.

Investigate the desk area	Turn to **87**
Investigate the open manual	Turn to **137**
Check out the half-eaten food	Turn to **79**

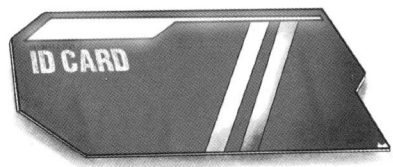

177

You move quickly left along the tunnel, out of line-of-sight from above. The vent continues for about thirty feet before stopping at a grate.

Try and force the grate	Turn to **44**
Head back along the corridor	Turn to **118**

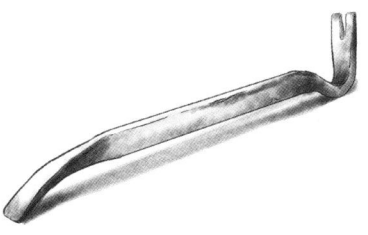

178

You enter the bridge and there are alarms going off all over the place. It's not a large room, but does house three seats, occupied by three bodies.

Roll 2d6 and test for *Detection*.

If the test is successful, turn to **46**. Otherwise, turn to **161**.

179

The bridge door closes behind you, but you know you haven't got long until the crew member reaches you.

You scan the room; there are three chairs in all, two of which house bodies, the right most one is empty.

There are screens blinking away, and few places to hide.

If you have a proximity mine and want to use it	Turn to **112**
If you have a blaster and want to use it	Turn to **157**
If you have pesticide and want to use it	Turn to **104**
Wait and face the crew member	Turn to **47**
Check the ship controls	Turn to **86**

180

You managed to manoeuvre into the small space between the engines.

You hear the elevator door open, and footsteps leading up to the engine room. The door opens and you hold your breath. Fortunately, the door closes, and you hear footsteps walking away.

You emerge from the space and think about your next move.

Now, turn to **84**.

181

The time has come to try something risky. You ready the blaster and fire.

Roll 2d6 and test for *Accuracy*.

If the test is successful, turn to **97**. Otherwise, turn to **123**.

182

Most of the surface seems clean, apart from the section at the far end, which has something disassembled on it.

There are cupboards above and below the sink.

Check out the disassembled gizmo at the end	Turn to **124**
Open the cupboard above the sink	Turn to **48**
Open the cupboard below the sink	Turn to **103**
Check out the half-eaten food	Turn to **79**
Investigate the desk area	Turn to **87**

183

You check the drawers, which are locked. There is a keyhole at the top of them.

Did you find a silver key?

If so, and want to try it, turn to **64**. Otherwise, turn to **128**.

184

You crawl away, but not nearly fast enough to escape some of the gas.

Deduct 4 from your *Health*.

Head left along the tunnel, turn to **136**.

185

You go towards the gizmo, but your suit catches in the lower cupboard door, opening it for a second. As soon as the seal is broken however, a swarm of Billut Bugs fly out. These are ravenous beasts with a sharp set of teeth. You must keep away from them.

Do you have a Sprayer?

If so, turn to **146**. Otherwise, turn to **67**.

186

Do you have a keycard?

If so, turn to **154**. Otherwise, turn to **129**.

187

You try the door to Engineering but it's locked. Not only that, but the lock mechanism has been hit with a blaster bolt, as if it's been sabotaged.

As you investigate, you hear the elevator whirr into life. Someone is coming down.

Check the engines door	Turn to **121**
Head towards the front	Turn to **156**
Try and sabotage the lift	Turn to **95**

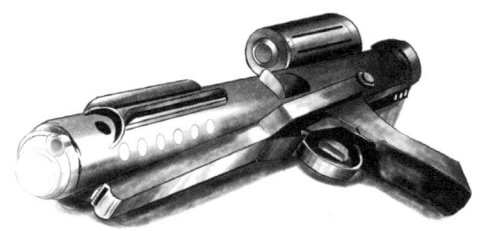

188

Nothing catches your eye, and as you are thinking about your next move, one of the terminals on the desks makes a noise.

Turn to **87**.

189

You flick through the pages of the manual but find nothing else.

As you think about your next move, one of the terminals on the desks makes a noise.

Turn to **87**.

190

One of them is completely bust, and has been harvested for parts, but the other one is just not plugged in.

You try and keep breathing the oxygen canister is empty. You fall to your knees gasping, feeling the poison burn your lungs. Fortunately, you lose consciousness with the second breath, and don't wake up.

191

The words 'Terminal locked for 27:03' are displayed and the numbers are counting down.

You try and keep breathing the oxygen canister is empty. You fall to your knees gasping, feeling the poison burn your lungs. Fortunately, you lose consciousness with the second breath, and don't wake up.

192

You reach down and plug the terminal in. The air in your oxygen tube is feeling a little thin, which gives you cause for concern.

The terminal powers up, and you see a 'Login:' prompt.

If you know a login id, go to the section number which equals the number in the ID.

193

You approach the nearest panel. It's flashing red and saying that there is gas on the ship. As you flip through the screens, you hear a noise behind you.

Roll 2d6 and test for *Speed*.

If the test is successful, turn to **115**. Otherwise, turn to **130**.

194

You go to check the other locker when you hear the enemy outside the door. The space outside is too small for them to use the blaster safely, but you hear another, high pitch, noise which sounds like a laser cutter.

Within seconds you see a hole open in the door, and then gas starts to enter the room.

Have you found a fresh gas mask and cylinder?

If so, turn to **91**. Otherwise, turn to **140**.

195

As you look at it, you hear the elevator whirr into life. Someone is coming down.

You notice the door to Engineering has been sabotaged and won't open.

Head towards the front	Turn to **156**
Try and sabotage the lift	Turn to **95**
Check the engines door	Turn to **121**

196

You search through the bunk but find nothing of any use.

Check the drawers	Turn to **183**
Open the door	Turn to **89**
Search the clothes	Turn to **128**

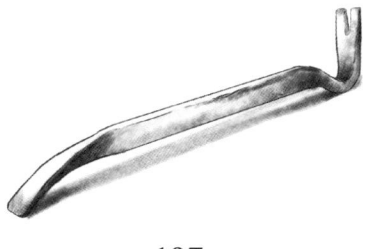

197

The bolt hits the perfect place, and the door is thrown backwards.

Are you wearing an oxygen mask?

If so, turn to **75**. Otherwise, turn to **110**.

198

Surprisingly, after a couple of dead ends, you manage to put it all back together (**+3w**). There's no liquid to put in it, however. The sink has water, so you could use that.

Add water to the canister	Turn to **175**
Investigate the open manual	Turn to **137**
Investigate the desk area	Turn to **87**
Open the cupboard above the sink	Turn to **48**
Open the cupboard below the sink	Turn to **103**
Check out the half-eaten food	Turn to **79**

199

With noises outside the door, you feel more under pressure than ever, but take a second to try and focus. Sweeping your hand over the floor you find a slightly higher panel than the others and immediately prise it up. You grab what's underneath and bring it closer to your face. It's a mask and fresh oxygen tank.

No sooner have you found it than you hear a hiss nearby and see gas coming in through a small hole in the door - they are trying to poison you. If you don't already have one you take the mask (**+4w**).

Turn to **91**.

200

You stand on the bridge with the fallen crew member before you. You take a moment to go over the events of the past hour, and still can't really believe it. Why did they want to kill you? Did they sabotage the ship?

The fact is you're unlikely to ever know.

What you do know is you're the last person alive on board. You briefly think about calling it in to the authorities, but you know they would just take the ship, and try and put the blame on you.

You decide to take the ship. You know some people who can alter the idents, make it yours, or just make it disappear entirely. You feel a rush of adrenaline as you realise you can go anywhere you want. Until your food and fuel run out.

You spend a while jettisoning the bodies and taking stock of what you have.

Two hours later you sit at the controls of your ship, a smile on your face. Your adventures are about to begin.

A Branching Narrative

Entombed!

Simon Birks

Entombed!

Welcome to the specific rules for Entombed!

These rules should be used in conjunction with the 'General Rules for Adventure' and will take precedence should there be a conflict between the two.

Additional Rules

You start the adventure with 25 *Health*.

You begin the adventure with no weapons.

You begin the adventure with no rations.

A Branching Narrative: Entombed!

1

You awake and everything is dark. The ground beneath you is cold and hard, and when you turn your hands over and press your fingers into it, it feels like stone. Not only, that, but your elbows scrape against more stone either side of you, and the air, well, there's nothing fresh about it.

You push yourself up onto your elbows, and the top of your head brushes the ceiling above. You raise your right hand and feel the stone above you. It's the same when you raise your knee and finally your foot. You are encased in stone.

Have you been buried alive? If so, there's little chance of getting out.

You lie back and press both arms against the coffin lid and push. It's hard work, but you do feel it shifting. Spurred on by the movement you redouble your efforts and slide the stone away, bracing yourself for the earth to fall in on you. Instead, you see another ceiling, a proper ceiling, about ten feet above you, and from the movement of the light, you can tell torches are lighting the room.

Carefully, you sit up and look around.

You are in an underground burial chamber. There are five other sarcophagi in the room, all closed. There is a statue of a demon with a quill and a scroll on a circular plinth in the centre of the room. To the wall on your left is a chest, and opposite you are a large, unlit hearth. There is an iron door diagonally opposite you which reminds you of a cell door. Several pots are placed around the room. On the wall behind you is a statue of a knight, to the right of which is a font. Lastly, on the wall over to the right, is a closed wooden door.

You climb out of your sarcophagus. You are dressed in a simple gown, which has seen better days.

What would you like to do?

Examine the knight	Turn to **7**
Investigate the chest	Turn to **11**
Try the iron door	Turn to **20**
Inspect the font	Turn to **24**
Search the pots	Turn to **41**
Look closely at the demon statue	Turn to **44**
Check the hearth	Turn to **87**
Explore the wooden door	Turn to **187**
Inspect the sarcophagi	Turn to **194**

2

You take a step forward carefully, without making a noise.

Again, a voice goes 'Sssshhhh!'

You take another step forward.

Roll 2d6 and test for *Stealth*.

If the test is successful, turn to **33**. Otherwise, turn to **22**.

3

Have you been able to light the kindling?

If so, turn to **54**. Otherwise, turn to **175**.

4

The door is locked and doesn't budge, however much you force it.

If you have a key, you could try to unlock it.

If you have a silver key	Turn to **23**
If you have a bronze key	Turn to **132**
If you have an iron key	Turn to **163**
If you have a wooden key	Turn to **32**
If you don't have a key	Turn to **116**

5

You retrieve the skull and throw it on the fire.

Now, turn to **17**.

6

You place the silver key in the lock and turn. A small compartment opens and inside you find a small web of light (**+0w**). A magical object for sure, for it weighs nothing when you take it.

Buoyed by your success, you turn to decide your next move.

Turn to **116**.

7

Have you found the web of light?

If so, turn to **177**. Otherwise, turn to **134**.

8

You eat the mushroom hoping to double its effects - unfortunately, nothing much changes, but you do develop a blinding headache, which impairs your concentration.

Reduce your *Detection* by 1.

The trapdoor shuts and you must now decide what to do (turn to **144**).

9

You slide the bronze key in and turn it. The mechanism clicks and the chest unlocks. Carefully, you lift the lid.

What position is the catch in?

The catch is up	Turn to **161**
The catch is down	Turn to **152**
What catch?	Turn to **94**

10

Carefully, you slide the catch up, bracing yourself. Nothing appears to happen,

Make a note the catch is up on your adventure sheet.

Try and move the chest	Turn to **45**
Try and open the chest	Turn to **74**
Look elsewhere	Turn to **116**

11

Have you already opened the chest?

If you have, turn to **86**. Otherwise, turn to **40**.

12

You attempt to reach in stealthily, but just as your hand is about to close around the skull, one of the rats runs out and nips your hand.

Deduct 2 from your *Health*.

You pull your hand out quickly without the skull - luckily for you as the trapdoor shuts with a snap.

Exit back into the main chamber	Turn to **116**
Take another look in the antechamber	Turn to **144**

13

Growing inside the hole are four mushrooms. One green, one yellow, one brown and one grey. You're no expert, but they may restore some of your *Health*.

Eat the green mushroom	Turn to **108**
Eat the brown mushroom	Turn to **53**
Eat the grey mushroom	Turn to **178**
Eat the yellow mushroom	Turn to **147**
Ignore the mushrooms	Turn to **69**

14

Have you altered the number of dice?

If you have, turn to **195**. Otherwise, turn to **125**.

15

Multiply the number of Stealth tests you just failed by 3 and take that much damage.

The rats scurry around and then back into the trapdoor.

Have you already found the skull?

If you have, turn to **183**. Otherwise, turn to **165**.

16

The first trapdoor opens behind you, and dart flies out, straight for you.

Roll 2d6 and test your *Speed*.

If the test is successful, turn to **159**. Otherwise, turn to **84**.

17

As soon as the object hits the flames, the fire flares up and catches you unawares.

Deduct 2 from your *Health*.

The object falls through the fire, and you pick it back up.

Throw something else on the fire	Turn to **54**
Ignore the fire and look elsewhere	Turn to **116**

18

You eat the mushroom, and after a moment everything sudden looks sharper.

Increase your *Accuracy* by 1.

The trapdoor closes, and you must decide your next move (turn to **144**).

19

You retrieve the pot of water and throw it on the fire. The water evaporates instantly, but nothing happens.

Throw something else on the fire	Turn to **54**
Ignore the fire and look elsewhere	Turn to **116**

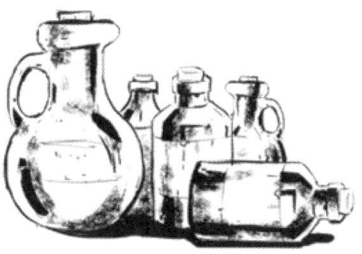

20

You make your way to the door, but it's locked with no sign of a keyhole. Through the bars you can see a corridor leading away with doors either side.

Have you inserted any objects into the door?

If you have, turn to **52**. Otherwise, turn to **112**.

21

Try as you might, you cannot find any catch.

Frustrated, you think through your options.

Try and move the chest	Turn to **45**
Try and open the chest	Turn to **74**
Look elsewhere	Turn to **116**

22

As you step forward your foot makes a noise against the floor and the trapdoor snaps shut.

Roll again	Turn to **164**
Return to the main chamber	Turn to **116**
Do something else in the antechamber	Turn to **144**

23

The silver key is far too small for the lock. You'll have to try something else.

If you have a bronze key	Turn to **132**
If you have an iron key	Turn to **163**
If you have a wooden key	Turn to **32**
Ignore the door and try something else	Turn to **116**

24

It looks like an ordinary font, with water constantly flowing into it from a hole in the wall. It has an outlet at the bottom which stops it overflowing.

If you have the black pot, you could collect some of the water, or you could drink some water out of your hands.

Collect water in the black pot	Turn to **110**
Drink from the font	Turn to **133**
Try something else	Turn to **116**

25

You reach in quickly, grab the skull (**+3w**) and pull your hand out before the trapdoor snaps shut.

Exit back to the main chamber	Turn to **116**
Take another look in the antechamber	Turn to **144**

26

You fall to the floor in a heap.

Deduct 2 from your *Health*.

You pick yourself up and turn to see what shoved you, but nothing is obvious.

As you watch, the trapdoor closes.

Turn to **144**.

27

There's movement from the corner of your eye and you turn just in time to see a figure made of smoke and fire coming out of the crack in the cross.

If you have a pot of water, turn to **123**. Otherwise, turn to **135**.

28

The second trapdoor opens, and out crawl three large eyeless rats, sniffing the air and listening.

Roll 2d6 and test for *Stealth* three times.

If all three tests are successful, turn to **131**. Otherwise, turn to **15**.

29

You retrieve the metal orb and throw it on the fire.

Now, turn to **157**.

30

You manage to avoid the clutches smoke monster and jump back through the doorway.

Roll 2d6 and test for *Accuracy*.

If the test is successful, turn to **126**. Otherwise, turn to **50**.

31

You reach in and grab the skull. As you pull it out, the trapdoor snaps down on your arm, making you let go of the skull.

Deduct 2 from your *Accuracy*.

You pull the trapdoor up with your free hand and manage to remove your arm, but only after the rats beneath the door have bitten your hand.

Deduct 3 from your *Health*.

Return to the main chamber	Turn to **116**
Take another look in the antechamber	Turn to **144**

32

You slot the key in the lock and turn. It moves slowly and you hear a click as the mechanism works.

You can keep the key.

You push open the door and walk in (turn to **37**).

33

You take a step forward carefully, without making a noise.

Again, a voice goes 'Sssshhhh!'

You take another step forward.

Roll 2d6 and test for *Stealth*.

If the test is successful, turn to **142**. Otherwise, turn to **103**.

34

Something doesn't seem right.

Roll 2d6 and test for *Detection*.

If the test is successful, turn to **70**. Otherwise, turn to **171**.

35

As you place the last tile in you feel a pain in your left leg.

Deduct 1 from your *Health*.

Fortunately, it subsides. Something about it felt like a warning.

Try another order	Turn to **92**
Search in the antechamber more	Turn to **144**
Go back through to the main chamber	Turn to **116**

36

As you place the last tile in you feel a pain in your right arm.

Deduct 1 from your *Health*.

Fortunately, it subsides. Something about it felt like a warning.

Try another order	Turn to **92**
Search in the antechamber more	Turn to **144**
Go back through to the main chamber	Turn to **116**

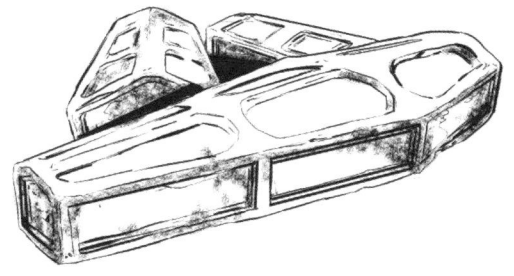

37

The antechamber has four trapdoors set into the floor. Off to the left is a stand with a wooden top holding some dice. There is a large stone cross next to the stand, and at the opposite end of the room, a stone tablet rests against the wall.

Go back to the main chamber	Turn to **116**
Look at something else in the antechamber	Turn to **144**

38

You manage to resist the temptation to throw the dice and the feeling passes.

What would you like to do?

Roll the dice, anyway	Turn to **164**
Return to the larger room	Turn to **116**
Look elsewhere in the antechamber	Turn to **144**

39

The fourth trapdoor opens.

Do you have the metal orb?

If so, turn to **193**. Otherwise, turn to **120**.

40

You make your way over to the chest. It is simply made, with a keyhole in the front, and a rope handle either side. You look down the back and underneath it but see nothing of note.

Try and open the chest	Turn to **74**
Try and move the chest	Turn to **45**
Look elsewhere	Turn to **116**

41

There are three pots in the room: a black one, a green one and a yellow one, all differing sizes.

Investigate the black pot	Turn to **185**
Investigate the yellow pot	Turn to **109**
Investigate the green pot	Turn to **150**
Look elsewhere	Turn to **116**

42

You retrieve the pot and throw it on the fire.

Now, turn to **17**.

43

The trapdoor shuts. You wait for something else to happen, but it doesn't.

Now, turn to **144**.

44

Have you picked up the candelabra yet?

If so, turn to **98**. Otherwise, turn to **57**.

45

You grab one of the rope handles and pull.

Roll 2d6 and test your *Power*.

If the test is successful, turn to **155**. Otherwise, turn to **79**.

46

The statue swings around and points at the sarcophagus in front of the hearth. You hear a click and the lid swings back.

You go over and look inside.

Do you already have the bronze key?

If you do, turn to **192**. Otherwise, turn to **65**.

47

You look around to see if there's anything you can use to force the door, but to no avail.

Frustrated, you turn to consider your options (turn to **116**).

48

As hard as you try you are unable to get the right weight, and you feel something sting the bottom of your foot.

You drop the pot as you nurse your wound.

Deduct 2 from your *Health*.

Investigate the black pot	Turn to **185**
Investigate the green pot	Turn to **150**
Try and pick the pot up again	Turn to **188**
Look elsewhere in the main chamber	Turn to **116**

49

You look at each of the sarcophagi and notice that each one bears a different number etched into the foot of the figure on top. The sarcophagus you were in has the number 2 on the foot, while the others have 3, 5, 7, 11, and 17. It's not certain what these numbers mean.

Sure these numbers must mean something, you look elsewhere (turn to **116**).

50

In your speed to evade the monster, you crack your head on the top of the door.

Deduct 2 from your *Health*.

Groggy you turn to see the smoke monster looking at you from the doorway. It appears it cannot come into this room. Relieved, you kick the door shut and decide your next move (turn to **116**).

51

Something triggers in your mind. You place the candelabra back on the plinth and the statue turns and the sarcophagus you were in unlocks. You pick it up again, and the demon moves to face the wooden chest.

You suppose the numbers on the sarcophagi are indicating the exact weight needed to unlock them.

Turn to **124**.

52

The spider-brooch sits in the door, next to the empty fly shaped indentation.

Do you have the iron fly? If so, turn to **136**. Otherwise, turn to **182**.

53

You eat the mushroom and, overall, feel a little better.

Restore 2 to your *Health*.

As you are about to choose another mushroom, the trapdoor closes. Turn to **144**.

54

The fire burns strongly in the hearth, giving off no heat.

Perhaps you can try and throw something onto the fire?

Throw a pot of water	Turn to **19**
Throw the skull	Turn to **5**
Throw the pot	Turn to **42**
Throw the die	Turn to **114**
Throw the spider-brooch	Turn to **81**
Throw the armour	Turn to **61**
Throw the metal orb	Turn to **29**
Throw the candelabra	Turn to **189**
Throw the rib	Turn to **104**
Ignore the fire and look elsewhere	Turn to **116**

55

You move slowly to the large stone cross. It looks out of place inside the room. There are cracks running up the structure, and you see two small images scratched into the surface. The first is wavy lines that might represent flames. The second is a circle.

You try to move the cross, but it seems stuck in place.

Return to the main chamber	Turn to **116**
Take another look in the antechamber	Turn to **144**

56

None of this makes much sense.

Frustrated, you decide to look elsewhere to find more clues.

Turn to **116**.

57

You walk towards the demon statue, checking the floor for any traps as you go. There don't seem to be any, and you're able to get close to the plinth supporting it.

One thing you immediately notice is that the top of the plinth seems to be on a mechanism which possibly makes the Demon able to rotate on the top to face different areas of the room. It's odd to say the least.

Currently there's a candelabra and candle resting on the plinth, and the demon appears to be looking at the sarcophagus you came out of.

Ignore the statue and look elsewhere	Turn to **116**
Pick up the candelabra	Turn to **196**

58

You place the silver key in the lock and turn. A jolt of electricity spasms your body.

It subsides, but leaves you shaken.

Reduce your *Stealth* by 1.

Try another keyhole	Turn to **160**
Ignore the knight and look elsewhere	Turn to **116**

59

You inspect the hearth but find nothing of importance.

Now, turn to **116**.

60

The statue swings around and points at the sarcophagus in front of the hearth. You hear a click and the lid swings back.

You go over and look inside.

Do you already have the wrist cuff?

If so, turn to **100**. Otherwise, turn to **181**.

61

You retrieve the armour and throw it on the fire.

Turn to **17**.

62

How would you like to try and light the kindling?

If you have any of the objects mentioned below, you can try them, otherwise you can look elsewhere.

Light the kindling with the candelabra	Turn to **148**
Light kindling with pot of water	Turn to **71**
Light kindling with nearby torch	Turn to **117**
Light kindling with Web of Light	Turn to **85**
Ignore the kindling and look elsewhere	Turn to **116**

63

Just before you put the water to your lips you notice a tingling sensation in your hands. You wait a moment, and it starts to burn. Quickly you drop the water on the floor.

Deduct 1 from your *Health*.

Collect water in the black pot	Turn to **110**
Look elsewhere	Turn to **116**

64

You bend and pick up the black pot (**+3w**) with ease. It's empty and you keep hold of it.

You are about to move away when you look down and see the black pot still on the ground. You check your inventory, and you still have your own one.

Confused by what just happened, and concerned for your own sanity, you ponder your next move.

Investigate the yellow pot	Turn to **109**
Investigate the green pot	Turn to **150**
Look elsewhere	Turn to **116**

65

You look inside the sarcophagus and find a bronze key (**+2w**).

Try and open another sarcophagus	Turn to **124**
Focus on other things in the room	Turn to **116**

66

You manage to dodge out the way as a spike shoot from the wall towards you. When you take your foot off the slab, the spike retracts back into the wall.

Thankful for your speed, you examine the knight (turn to **107**).

67

You place the silver key in the lock and turn. A jolt of electricity spasms your body.

It subsides, but leaves you shaken.

Reduce your *Accuracy* by 1.

Try another keyhole	Turn to **160**
Leave the knight and look elsewhere	Turn to **116**

68

You manage to stop yourself crashing to the floor and turn in time to see smoke being sucked back into the crack in the stone cross.

Turn to **144**.

69

After a moment the trapdoor closes, and you turn to work out your next move.

Turn to **144**.

70

The tablet doesn't look as flush to the wall as you'd expect. You look behind it and see something is jammed between it and the wall. You can't make out what it is.

Attempt to put the tiles in	Turn to **92**
Take another look in the antechamber	Turn to **144**
Go back to search the main chamber	Turn to **116**

71

Going against every ounce of experience you've gained, you pour the water on the kindling. Surprisingly, the kindling does smoke a little, but does not catch light, and before too long all the water has evaporated.

Light the kindling with the candelabra	Turn to **148**
Light kindling with nearby torch	Turn to **117**
Light kindling with Web of Light	Turn to **85**
Ignore the hearth and look elsewhere	Turn to **116**

72

And did you successfully detect anything on the sarcophagi?

If so, turn to **51**. Otherwise, turn to **56**.

73

The black pot is stuck to the floor, and no matter how hard you try to move it, it won't budge.

Investigate the yellow pot	Turn to **109**
Investigate the green pot	Turn to **150**
Look elsewhere	Turn to **116**

74

Carefully, you place your fingers under the lip of the lid and pull upwards. It doesn't budge. It appears to be locked. You look around for something to prise the lid open but see nothing obvious.

Have you found any keys you'd like to try to open it with?

If you haven't found a key	Turn to **83**
If you have an iron key	Turn to **88**
If you have a silver key	Turn to **130**
If you have a bronze key	Turn to **9**
If you have a wooden key	Turn to **118**

75

As you place the last tile in you feel a glow in your chest.

Restore 2 to your *Health*.

The feeling fades, and something about the experience felt like a message.

Try another order	Turn to **92**
Search in the antechamber more	Turn to **144**
Go back through to the main chamber	Turn to **116**

76

As you step forward your foot makes a noise against the floor and the trapdoor snaps shut.

Roll again	Turn to **164**
Go back through to the main chamber	Turn to **116**
Do something else in the antechamber	Turn to **144**

77

As you get nearer, something about the floor catches your eye and see a slightly raised flagstone. Looking around you notice a small hole in the wall which likely houses a dagger or dart of some kind.

You carefully step over it to look at the knight (turn to **107**).

78

The trapdoor isn't shutting quickly, but still, there's no point in hanging around to retrieve the skull.

Roll 2d6 and test for *Speed*.

If the test is successful, turn to **128**. Otherwise, turn to **31**.

79

You attempt to move the chest, but quickly realise there is more than just gravity holding it in place.

Annoyed, you give up.

Try and open the chest	Turn to **74**
Look elsewhere in the main chamber	Turn to **116**

80

As you place the last tile in you feel a pain in your right leg.

Deduct 1 from your *Health*.

Fortunately, it subsides. Something about it felt like a warning.

Try another order	Turn to **92**
Search in the antechamber more	Turn to **144**
Go back through to the main chamber	Turn to **116**

81

You retrieve the spider-brooch and throw it on the fire.

Turn to **17**.

82

The trapdoor hits your arm as you pull it out emptyhanded.

Deduct 2 from your *Accuracy*.

Roll again	Turn to **164**
Return to the main chamber	Turn to **116**
Do something else in the antechamber	Turn to **144**

83

Without a key, you can either check for hidden catches, attempt to move the chest, or look elsewhere.

Check for hidden catches	Turn to **156**
Attempt to move the chest	Turn to **45**
Look elsewhere in the main chamber	Turn to **116**

84

Before you have a chance to dodge it, the dart hits you.

Deduct 2 from your *Health*.

The trapdoor shuts as you nurse your wounds.

Take another look in the antechamber	Turn to **144**
Exit into the larger room	Turn to **116**

85

You put the web of light on top of the kindling, and instantly it catches, and the fire roars up in front of you, though gives off no heat. It appears these are magical flames.

Turn to **54**.

86

The chest is open and empty. You look to see if it holds any more secrets, but you find nothing.

Turn to **116**.

87

You approach the hearth, looking around for any potential traps, and are relieved when you make it there safely.

Have you placed any kindling in the hearth?

If so, turn to **3**. Otherwise, turn to **102**.

88

You try the iron key in the lock but, while it fits, it doesn't turn.

If you have another key, you could try that, you could attempt to move the chest, search for a hidden catch, or look elsewhere?

Try the silver key	Turn to **130**
Try the bronze key	Turn to **9**
Try and move the chest	Turn to **45**
Search for hidden catches	Turn to **156**
If you have a wooden key	Turn to **118**
Look elsewhere	Turn to **116**

89

The trapdoor grazes your arm as you pull it out emptyhanded.

Deduct 1 from your *Accuracy*.

Roll again	Turn to **164**
Return to the main chamber	Turn to **116**
Look for something else in the antechamber	Turn to **144**

90

The trapdoor isn't shutting quickly, so carefully you reach in to retrieve the skull.

Roll 2d6 and test for *Stealth*.

If the test is successful, turn to **121**. Otherwise, turn to **12**.

91

Something doesn't seem quite right.

Roll 2d6 and test for *Detection*.

If the test is successful, turn to **27**. Otherwise, turn to **145**.

92

What order would you like to choose?

Fox, Snake, Cat	Turn to **35**
Fox, Cat, Snake	Turn to **80**
Snake, Fox, Cat	Turn to **75**
Snake, Cat, Fox	Turn to **166**
Cat, Fox, Snake	Turn to **139**
Cat, Snake, Fox	Turn to **36**

93

You push as hard as you can and rock the pot, but you lose your balance, and the pot catches your hand against the wall.

Reduce your *Accuracy* by 1.

Investigate the yellow pot	Turn to **109**
Investigate the black pot	Turn to **185**
Look elsewhere	Turn to **116**

94

You lift the lid slowly, and are relieved when nothing happens, at first. After a few moments, a thin jet of green gas shoots at you from the back right of the chest.

Deduct 2 from your *Health*.

Inside the chest is some kindling wood (**+5w**). It glistens slightly in the torchlight, making you think it's not normal kindling. You take it, add it to your equipment list.

Now, turn to **116**.

95

The statue swings around and points at the sarcophagus in front of the hearth. You hear a click and the lid swings back.

You go over and look inside.

Do you already have the extra die?

If so, turn to **191**. Otherwise, turn to **105**.

96

You find nothing but stale air inside the sarcophagus.

Try and open another sarcophagus	Turn to **124**
Focus on other things in the room	Turn to **116**

97

You lift the pot without problem. On the bottom is a message scrawled in what might be blood.

It reads, 'You will need another die.'

Unsure of what it means, you replace the pot.

Investigate the black pot	Turn to **185**
Investigate the green pot	Turn to **150**
Look elsewhere in the main chamber	Turn to **116**

98

The demon statue is pointing towards the wooden chest.

Have you inspected the sarcophagi yet?

If so, turn to **72**. Otherwise, turn to **56**.

99

You place the silver key in the lock and turn. A jolt of electricity spasms your body.

It subsides, but leaves you shaken.

Reduce your *Accuracy* by 1.

Try another keyhole	Turn to **160**
Ignore the knight and look elsewhere	Turn to **116**

100

You find nothing but stale air inside the sarcophagus.

Try and open another sarcophagus	Turn to **124**
Focus on other things in the room	Turn to **116**

101

You look inside the sarcophagus and find a wooden key (**+1w**).

Try and open another sarcophagus	Turn to **124**
Focus on other things in the room	Turn to **116**

102

The hearth doesn't look overly special, but you notice there is no kindling or wood to set a fire. You check the bricks at the back to see if any are false but find nothing.

Do you have kindling for the hearth?

If so, turn to **138**. Otherwise, turn to **59**.

103

As you step forward your foot makes a noise against the floor and the trapdoor snaps shut.

Roll again	Turn to **164**
Go back to the main chamber	Turn to **116**
Do something else in the antechamber	Turn to **144**

104

You retrieve the rib and throw it on the fire.

Turn to **17**.

105

You look inside the sarcophagus and find an extra die (**+0w**).

Try and open another sarcophagus	Turn to **124**
Focus on other things in the room	Turn to **116**

106

"I will swap it for something you need," says the voice. "Throw the key in the hole."

Do you have the silver key?

If so, turn to **91**. Otherwise, turn to **146**.

107

You search the knight to see what secrets it yields and find five small silver keyholes.

Do you have a silver key?

If so, and you would like to use it, turn to **160**. Otherwise, turn to **140**.

108

You eat the green mushroom and hope it's not poisonous. After a few moments you see a glow surrounding the stone tablet. The patterns on the tablet swirl until you see a totem form with an owl at the top, on top of a cat, on top of a fox, on top of a snake.

The vision only lasts for a few seconds before vanishing.

The trapdoor closes and you must decide your next move.

Turn to **144**.

109

The yellow pot is cracked with several holes in its main body.

Pick the pot up	Turn to **180**
Investigate the black pot	Turn to **185**
Investigate the green pot	Turn to **150**
Look elsewhere in the main chamber	Turn to **116**

110

You dip the black pot into the water and fill it up.

The full black pot now has a weight of (**+6w**). Make a note of it on your equipment sheet.

Drink water from the font	Turn to **133**
Look elsewhere in the main chamber	Turn to **116**

111

You place the silver key in the lock and turn. A jolt of electricity spasms your body.

It subsides, but leaves you shaken.

Reduce your *Stealth* by 1.

Try another keyhole	Turn to **160**
Ignore the knight and look elsewhere	Turn to **116**

112

There's not much surface to look at, but you do notice an indentation in the shape of a spider.

Do you have a spider-shaped object?

If so, turn to **169**. Otherwise, turn to **47**.

113

The third trapdoor opens. You wait to see if anything is going to come out of it, but all is quiet. Suddenly, you hear a voice.

"Do you have the silver key?"

Say "I do have the key."	Turn to **106**
Say "I don't have the key."	Turn to **43**

114

You retrieve the die and throw it on the fire.

Turn to **17**.

115

Carefully, you slide the catch down, bracing yourself. Nothing appears to happen.

Make a note the catch is down on your adventure sheet.

Try and move the chest	Turn to **45**
Try and open the chest	Turn to **74**
Look elsewhere in the chamber	Turn to **116**

116

You scan the large burial chamber to try and work out what you should do next.

Investigate the chest	Turn to **11**
Check the hearth	Turn to **87**
Explore the wooden door	Turn to **187**
Try the iron door	Turn to **20**
Look closely at the Demon statue	Turn to **44**
Examine the knight	Turn to **7**
Inspect the sarcophagi	Turn to **194**
Search the pots	Turn to **41**
Inspect the font	Turn to **24**

117

You reach up to take the nearest burning torch.

Roll 2d6 and test for *Detection*.
If the test is successful, turn to **137**. Otherwise, turn to **179**.

118

The wooden key is far too large for the keyhole.

If you have another key, you could try that, you could attempt to move the chest, search for a hidden catch, or look elsewhere?

If you have a bronze key	Turn to **9**
Try and move the chest	Turn to **45**
If you have an iron key	Turn to **88**
If you have a silver key	Turn to **130**
Check for hidden catches	Turn to **156**
Look elsewhere in the chamber	Turn to **116**

119

The water covers the creature, and it screams in pain and recoils back into the crack.

Turn to **149**.

120

You can't be sure, but you think you hear something saying 'Ssshhh!' from within.

Slightly concerned, you wait a moment in case it's boobytrapped. When nothing happens, you take a step forward carefully.

Roll 2d6 and test your *Stealth*.

If the test is successful, turn to **2**. Otherwise, turn to **76**.

121

Carefully, you reach in and put your hand around the skull. As you pull it out the door snaps shut and clips your arm.

Deduct 1 from your *Accuracy*.

Deduct 1 from your *Health*.

Exit back into the main chamber	Turn to **116**
Take another look in the antechamber	Turn to **144**

122

You move your hands over the chest, trying to find any catches or raised areas which might indicate another way of getting in. You're about to give up when your hand brushes something on the back right of the container.

It feels like a catch that can either slide up or down.

Slide the catch-up	Turn to **10**
Slide the catch down	Turn to **115**
Try and move the chest	Turn to **45**
Look elsewhere in the chamber	Turn to **116**

123

You throw the water at the creature.

Roll 2d6 and test for *Accuracy*.

If the test is successful, turn to **119**. Otherwise, turn to **141**.

124

If you can, you can use items from your equipment list which you've picked up to make up the numbers on the sarcophagi.

Place items exactly matching 1w	Turn to **60**
Place items exactly matching 5w	Turn to **151**
Place items exactly matching 13w	Turn to **46**
Place items exactly matching 11w	Turn to **176**
Place items exactly matching 17w	Turn to **95**
Ignore the sarcophagi and look elsewhere	Turn to **116**

125

On the top of the stone stand is a wooden bowl with three dice. You push the dice around and pick one up. They look like perfectly normal dice.

You get a sudden urge to roll the dice.

Roll 2d6 and test for *Power*.

If the test is successful, turn to **38**. Otherwise, turn to **164**.

126

You duck your head as you go through the door, spin and slam the door shut behind you.

You expect the monster to continue its attack, but apart from a solitary roar, you hear no more.

You take a second to recover your breath and stand to plan your next move.

Turn to **116**.

127

You search the figures for more information but find nothing.

A little confused by the sarcophagi, you decide to look elsewhere.

Turn to **116**.

128

You reach in quickly.

Roll 2d6 and test for *Accuracy*.

If the test is successful, turn to **25**. Otherwise, turn to **197**.

129

You see the pattern clearly before the trapdoor shuts. It depicts a switch of some kind, with a cross at the top at a tick at the bottom.

The trapdoor closes and you must choose what to do.

Exit into the main chamber	Turn to **116**
Take another look in the antechamber	Turn to **144**

130

The silver key is far too small for the keyhole.

If you have another key, you could try that, you could attempt to move the chest, search for a hidden catch, or look elsewhere?

Try the iron key	Turn to **88**
Try the bronze key	Turn to **9**
Try the wooden key	Turn to **118**
Search for hidden catches	Turn to **156**
Try and move the chest	Turn to **45**
Look elsewhere in the main chamber	Turn to **116**

131

You avoid the rats and after a minute they crawl back into the trapdoor and disappear out of sight.

Have you already found the skull?

If so, turn to **183**. Otherwise, turn to **165**.

132

The bronze key is slightly too small for the lock and doesn't turn. You'll have to try something else.

If you have a silver key	Turn to **23**
If you have an iron key	Turn to **163**
If you have a wooden key	Turn to **32**
Ignore the door and look elsewhere	Turn to **116**

133

You cup your hand and scoop up some of the water. It feels cold to your hands.

Roll 2d6 and test for *Detection*.

If the test is successful, turn to **63**. Otherwise, turn to **199**.

134

You approach the stone knight carefully, actively looking for traps.

Roll 2d6 and test for *Detection*.

If the test is successful, turn to **77**. Otherwise, turn to **172**.

135

You jump towards the door back to the main chamber.

Roll 2d6 and test your *Speed*.

If you are successful, turn to **30**. Otherwise, turn to **158**.

136

You place the iron fly in the indentation. Much like the spider-brooch before it, the fly becomes part of the door, and both the spider and the fly glow. After a second there's a click and the door swings slightly ajar.

Now, turn to **200**.

137

You feel a sense of underlying foreboding as your hand grows closer to the torch.

Maybe it's not such a good idea.

Reach up and take the torch, anyway	Turn to **179**
Light the kindling with the candelabra	Turn to **148**
Light kindling with pot of water	Turn to **71**
Light kindling with Web of Light	Turn to **85**
Ignore the hearth and look elsewhere	Turn to **116**

138

You place the kindling on the hearth and step back. You're not sure if you were expecting something to happen, but nothing does.

You can try and light the kindling something you have in your inventory, or you can continue your search.

    Continue your search   Turn to **116**
    Try and light the kindling   Turn to **62**

139

You put the tiles in, and the tablet swings forward. Looking behind the tablet you find a rib bone (**+2w**).

There doesn't seem to be anything else remarkable about the tablet.

    Search in the antechamber more   Turn to **144**
    Go back through to the main chamber   Turn to **116**

140

Apart from the keyholes, the knight holds nothing of interest.

You must ponder your next move.

Turn to **116**.

141

The water partially hits the monster, causing it to recoil. This gives you enough time to dart through the doorway into the other room.

You pull the door closed behind you, expecting the monster to continue its attack, but apart from a solitary roar, you hear no more.

You take a second to recover your breath and stand to plan your next move.

Turn to **116**.

142

You can now see inside the trapdoor and can see a metal orb on the ground inside.

Once more, a voice says 'Sssshhhhh!'

Roll 2d6 and test for *Stealth*.

If the test is successful, turn to **162**. Otherwise, turn to **167**.

143

You brace yourself to move the pot.

Roll 2d6 and test for *Power*.

If the test is successful, turn to **153**. Otherwise, turn to **93**.

144

You can now do any of the following.

Check the stand	Turn to **14**
Inspect the trapdoors	Turn to **174**
Look at the stone cross	Turn to **55**
Approach the stone tablet	Turn to **186**
Go back to the main chamber	Turn to **116**

145

You wait for a response, but before you receive one, something knocks you off your feet.

Deduct 3 from your *Health*.

You turn to see a monster of smoke and fire coming towards you.

You move backwards and get to your feet.

Do you have a pot filled with water?

If so, turn to **123**. Otherwise, turn to **135**.

146

The voice replies 'Liar' and you feel a shove in your back, sending you tumbling forwards.

Roll 2d6 and test your *Accuracy*.

Roll 2d6 and test your *Speed*.

If both tests are successful, turn to **68**. Otherwise, turn to **26**.

147

Have you eaten a yellow mushroom previously?

If so, turn to **8**. Otherwise, turn to **18**.

148

You place the flame of the candelabra on the top of the kindling and wait. Annoyingly, nothing happens. It appears the kindling can't be lit by normal means.

Light kindling with pot of water	Turn to **71**
Light kindling with nearby torch	Turn to **117**
Light kindling with Web of Light	Turn to **85**
Ignore the hearth and look elsewhere	Turn to **116**

149

Do you have the silver key?

If so, turn to **13**. Otherwise, turn to **173**.

150

The green pot looks heavy, and you wouldn't be able to carry it around.

Move the pot	Turn to **143**
Investigate the yellow pot	Turn to **109**
Investigate the black pot	Turn to **185**
Look elsewhere in the chamber	Turn to **116**

151

The statue swings around and points at the sarcophagus in front of the hearth. You hear a click and the lid swings back.

You go over and look inside.

Do you already have the wooden key?

If so, turn to **96**. Otherwise, turn to **101**.

152

You lift the lid slowly and are relieved when nothing happens.

Inside the chest is some kindling wood (**+5w**). It glistens slightly in the torchlight, making you think it's not normal kindling. You take it, add it to your equipment list.

Turn to **116**.

153

After a lot of straining, you roll the pot a little way, but it reveals nothing underneath.

Investigate the black pot	Turn to **185**
Investigate the yellow pot	Turn to **109**
Look elsewhere in the chamber	Turn to **116**

154

A spike shoots from the wall and you can do nothing to get out of its way. It punctures your skin.

Deduct 3 from your *Health*.

Cursing your stupidity, you look closely at the knight (turn to **107**).

155

You put everything you have into moving the chest, and you think you feel it shift a fraction, but no further. You're exhausted from the exertion.

Reduce your *Health* by 1.

Try and open the chest	Turn to **74**
Look elsewhere in the chamber	Turn to **116**

156

Carefully, you run your hands over the surface of the chest.

Roll 2d6 and test for *Detection*.

If the test is successful, turn to **122**. Otherwise, turn to **21**.

157

The flames instantly start melting the orb and after a few seconds a tiny iron fly (**+2w**) falls to the floor beneath the fire. You pick the iron fly up.

You turn and ponder your next move.

Turn to **116**.

158

As fast as you move, the smoke monster seems to be quicker. It catches you back before you have chance to make it through the door.

Deduct 3 from your *Health*.

You stumble through the door and kick it shut behind you. You expect the monster to continue its attack, but apart from a solitary roar, you hear no more.

You take a second to recover your breath and stand to plan your next move.

Turn to **116**.

159

Just as the dart is about to hit, you jink out of the way, and it embeds itself into the wall behind you and disappears.

There is something on the back of the trapdoor.

Roll 2d6 and test for *Speed*.

If the test is successful, turn to **129**. Otherwise, turn to **184**.

160

You have the choice to open any of the five compartments.

Try the left arm keyhole	Turn to **67**
Try the right arm keyhole	Turn to **99**
Try the chest keyhole	Turn to **6**
Try the left leg keyhole	Turn to **58**
Try the right leg keyhole	Turn to **111**
Ignore the keyholes and look elsewhere	Turn to **116**

161

You lift the lid slowly, and are relieved when nothing happens, at first. After a few moments, a thick jet of green gas shoots at you from the back right of the chest.

Deduct 4 from your *Health*.

Inside the chest is some kindling wood (**+5w**). It glistens slightly in the torchlight, making you think it's not normal kindling. You take it, add it to your equipment list.

Now, turn to **116**.

162

You reach in carefully and retrieve the metal orb (**+3w**).

As you move your arm out, the trapdoor shuts.

Go back to the main chamber	Turn to **116**
Check out the antechamber	Turn to **144**

163

The iron key fits into the lock but doesn't turn. You'll have to try something else.

If you have a silver key	Turn to **23**
If you have a bronze key	Turn to **132**
If you have a wooden key	Turn to **32**
Ignore the door and look elsewhere	Turn to **116**

164

You pick up the dice and roll them. Roll the same number of d6 as were in the bowl, add up the total, and turn to the section indicated below.

Total between 1 and 6	Turn to **16**
Total between 7 and 12	Turn to **28**
Total between 13 and 18	Turn to **113**
Total between 19 and 24	Turn to **39**

165

As the trapdoor begins to close you see a skull in the darkness below.

What would you like to do?

Use Stealth to try and retrieve it	Turn to **90**
Use Speed to try and retrieve it	Turn to **78**
Ignore it	Turn to **183**

166

As you place the last tile in you feel a pain in your left arm.

Deduct 1 from your *Health*.

Fortunately, it subsides. Something about it felt like a warning.

Try another order	Turn to **92**
Search in the antechamber more	Turn to **144**
Go back through to the main chamber	Turn to **116**

167

You reach in to take the orb, but suddenly overbalance and make a noise. The trapdoor snaps shut.

Roll 2d6 and test for *Speed*.

If the test is successful, turn to **89**. Otherwise, turn to **82**.

168

As soon as you begin to lift the pot you feel something sting the bottom of your foot.

You drop the pot as you nurse your wound.

Deduct 2 from your *Health*.

Try to pick the pot up again	Turn to **180**
Investigate the black pot	Turn to **185**
Investigate the green pot	Turn to **150**
Look elsewhere in the chamber	Turn to **116**

169

You place the spider-brooch in the indentation, and it immediately becomes part of the door, and next to it another indentation appears in the shape of a fly.

Do you have a fly shaped object?

If so, turn to **136**. Otherwise, turn to **182**.

170

You find nothing but stale air inside the sarcophagus.

Try and open another sarcophagus	Turn to **124**
Focus on other things in the room	Turn to **116**

171

You don't notice anything specific.

Attempt to put the tiles in	Turn to **92**
Go back to the main chamber	Turn to **116**
Look at something else in the antechamber	Turn to **144**

172

You are about to reach the Knight when you step on a flagstone which dips under your weight.

Roll 2d6 and test for *Speed*.

If the test is successful, turn to **66**. Otherwise, turn to **154**.

173

You peer into the hole. Hovering unaided in the hole is a silver key (+0w). You take it, momentarily confused, as it appears to weigh nothing.

You secure it in your pocket and watch as the trapdoor closes.

Turn to **144**.

174

There are four trapdoors, one behind another, all of them shut. They all bear an emblem of a skull. There's no way to force them up.

Go back to the main chamber	Turn to **116**
Take another look in the antechamber	Turn to **144**

175

You can try and light the kindling or ignore the hearth and look elsewhere.

Try and light the kindling	Turn to **62**
Look elsewhere in the main chamber	Turn to **116**

176

The statue swings around and points at the sarcophagus in front of the hearth. You hear a click and the lid swings back.

You go over and look inside.

Do you already have the spider-brooch?

If so, turn to **170**. Otherwise, turn to **190**.

177

The knight has an open, empty compartment in his chest, but nothing else of note.

Turn to **116**.

178

You eat the grey mushroom and wait to see what happens. The trapdoor closes in front of you, and you are about to see what you should do next when a pain explodes in your stomach, causing you to double over in pain.

It doesn't last long, but when it subsides, you don't feel as good as before.

Deduct 2 from your *Health*.

Now, turn to **144**.

179

As you put your hand on the handle of the torch you feel a jolt of coldness down your arm. You let go immediately.

Reduce your *Accuracy* by 1.

Light the kindling with the candelabra	Turn to **148**
Light kindling with pot of water	Turn to **71**
Light kindling with Web of Light	Turn to **85**
Ignore the hearth and look elsewhere	Turn to **116**

180

You bend to pick the pot up.

Roll 2d6 and test for *Detection*.

If the test is successful, turn to **198**. Otherwise, turn to **168**.

181

You look inside the sarcophagus and find a steel wrist cuff (**+4w**) in a bad state.

Try and open another sarcophagus	Turn to **124**
Focus on other things in the room	Turn to **116**

182

You look around to see if there's anything you can use to force the door, but to no avail.

Frustrated, you turn to consider your options.

Turn to **116**.

183

The trapdoor slowly closes then snaps shut.

Exit back into the main chamber	Turn to **116**
Take another look in the antechamber	Turn to **144**

184

You try and make out what's on the back of the trapdoor, but it closes too quickly.

Exit into the larger room	Turn to **116**
Take another look in the antechamber	Turn to **144**

185

Do you already own a black pot?

If so, turn to **73**. Otherwise, turn to **64**.

186

There are three spaces aligned vertically in the stone tablet underneath a tile of an owl, and three tiles laid out in front of it.

One is a cat, another a fox, and the last is a snake. The tiles will fit in the spaces.

Attempt to put the tiles in	Turn to **92**
Search for a clue as to their order	Turn to **34**
Go back to the main chamber	Turn to **116**
Look at something else in the antechamber	Turn to **144**

187

Have you unlocked the door?

If so, turn to **37**. Otherwise, turn to **4**.

188

You try and apply the same pressure to the floor, equal to the weight of the pot, as you lift it.

Roll 2d6 and test for *Accuracy*.

If the test is successful, turn to **97**. Otherwise, turn to **48**.

189

You retrieve the candelabra and throw it on the fire.

Turn to **17**.

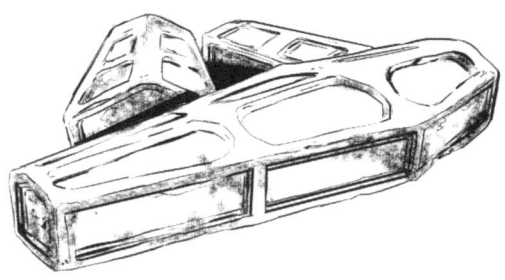

190

You look inside the sarcophagus and find a spider-brooch (**+2w**).

Try and open another sarcophagus	Turn to **124**
Focus on other things in the room	Turn to **116**

191

You find nothing but stale air inside the sarcophagus.

Try and open another sarcophagus	Turn to **124**
Focus on other things in the room	Turn to **116**

192

You find nothing but stale air inside the sarcophagus.

Try and open another sarcophagus	Turn to **124**
Focus on other things in the room	Turn to **116**

193

There's no need to play this game. You make a noise and the trapdoor shuts.

Roll again	Turn to **164**
Return to the main chamber	Turn to **116**
Do something else in the antechamber	Turn to **144**

194

You look at each of the sarcophagi. They all bear a figure on top, with various symbols around the base.

You attempt to move the lid each of the sarcophagi, but they are held in place by more than just their weight.

You can't help feeling your missing something important.

Roll 2d6 and test for *Detection*.

If the test is successful, turn to **49**. Otherwise, turn to **127**.

195

On the top of the stone stand is a wooden bowl with four dice. You push the dice around and pick one up. They look like perfectly normal dice.

You get a sudden urge to roll the dice.

Roll 2d6 and test for *Power*.

If the test is successful, turn to **38**. Otherwise, turn to **164**.

196

You pick up the candelabra (**+2w**), ready for something to happen, and it does. The lid of the sarcophagus you were in swings shut and the statue moves to stare at the wooden chest against the wall.

Have you inspected the sarcophagi yet?

If so, turn to **72**. Otherwise, turn to **56**.

197

You attempt to reach in quickly but your hand misses and is bitten by one of the rats.

Deduct 1 from your *Health*.

You pull your hand out quickly without the skull - luckily for you as the trapdoor shuts with a snap.

Exit to the main chamber	Turn to **116**
Take another look in the antechamber	Turn to **144**

198

You notice the pot is resting on a raised piece of ground, which might signify a trap.

You can still lift the pot, but you'll have to be careful.

Lift the pot	Turn to **188**
Investigate the black pot	Turn to **185**
Investigate the green pot	Turn to **150**
Look elsewhere in the main chamber	Turn to **116**

199

You gulp the water down, and after a moment, start to feel it burn inside you. You stick your fingers down your throat and throw the water back up, but not before it's done considerable damage.

Deduct 5 from your *Health*.

Collect water in the black pot	Turn to **110**
Look elsewhere	Turn to **116**

200

You push the door open and step outside. Congratulations, you've escaped!